Storm Rising

Steven Becker

Storm Rising

This is a work of fiction. Names, characters, places and incidents either are the product of the author's imagination or are used fictitiously . Any resemblance to any persons, living or dead, events or locales is entirely coincidental.

steve@stevenbeckerauthor.com
Stevenbeckerauthor.com

Storm Rising

CHAPTER 1

Mako leaned against the bar, carefully surveying the crowd, one hand on his pint, the other mindlessly caressing the smooth mahogany. He should have been watching the street, but he was distracted and chose to admire the women instead. Exchanging glances with several, he smiled and met their eyes, challenging those with escorts, inviting those without. One woman in particular caught his attention, her large blue eyes meeting his over the shoulder of her boyfriend. Her body language gave a clear signal that she would prefer his company. A flash of chrome forced his eyes away, and with an effort he moved his gaze to the street. Smiling at his luck, he grabbed his phone from the bar. *Pulling up at Harrods*, he typed and drained the beer.

"This is our chance," Alicia's voice said in his ear.

"On my way," he whispered into the flesh-colored bone induction mike and walked out the door. Fingering the GPS chip in his pocket, he scanned the street looking for the metallic cherry red "G" class Mercedes. The large city block that was Harrods department store came into view, and he saw the extended-cab SUV illegally parked at the corner. "Got it."

Not knowing if the vehicle was driven by the owner, a high-level Iranian diplomat, or his chauffeur, Mako slowed as he approached, trying to blend in with the other tourists who gawked at the unique vehicle or took pictures of it with their phones. He moved toward the SUV, trying to find the angle from which the sun would allow him to see inside the heavily-tinted windows. It was empty. He breathed deeply and closed the gap. With the chip in one hand, he withdrew a small ball of putty from his pocket and started working it with the fingers of his other hand. The materials combined, and when he felt the heat caused by the chemical reaction, he used his thumb to attach it to the chip. A group of teenagers were hanging around the SUV, using it as a backdrop for a picture, when he moved to the curb and ducked by the rear wheel. They struck a provocative pose, and he used the distraction to lean over and stick the chip to the inside of the wheel well.

Minutes later, he was back in the pub with another pint in front of him, his attention now entirely on the crowd. The woman he had made eye contact with before stood, and he thought for a second about following, but the voice was back in his head.

"It's good. I have a signal," Alicia said.

"Of course," he muttered back.

"Really, you're back in the pub? We have work to do."

He really wished she had a sexier voice, but as far as partners went, she was first-class. Instead of replying, he texted her. *Just let me know when he is at the target.* With a practiced movement, he removed the earwig and placed it discreetly in his pocket, hoping he could take care of this bit of business and have a few days to enjoy the London scene. The woman's seat was still empty, and he decided to take a chance. Leaving his half-finished pint on the bar, he made his way through the crowd, finding himself in the vestibule by the bathrooms. Disappointed she was not there, he made a move to the men's room, when a hand reached out and pulled him close. Without a word, he felt her lips brush against his face and her tongue enter his mouth.

She broke off the kiss. "Your phone," she said with a smile. Without waiting, she brushed her hand against his pants pockets and pulled out the phone.

He leaned in close as she started to enter her phone number in a new text window. Suddenly the phone vibrated and she stopped, two digits short.

"Looks like you have something more important," she said and handed it back to him.

Still looking at her, he glanced down at the new message. *Find something better than me? He's on the move and heading in the right direction.*

"Sorry, love," Mako said and brought his face toward her, but she expertly slid under his arm and was gone. Although she might have been intriguing, he let her go and slid between the bodies layered two deep at the bar, making his way to the exit. On his way out the door, he cast a look back at her table and saw her purposefully reach for her boyfriend and kiss him. She sensed him watching and he caught her eye with a wink.

Brompton Road was wall to wall with tourists and traffic, so he cut over a block to Basil Street. Increasing his pace, he evaded the tourists exiting the Knightsbridge tube station and started walking down the escalator. A couple taking up the entire width stopped him, and he was forced to wait for the mechanized stairs to descend. His phone buzzed with another text. *I know I'm not in your head—can you fix that?* He realized he had not replaced the earwig and dug in his pockets for the small device. When it was not in the right front, he panicked, thinking that the woman had taken it, but he patted his left pocket and felt the small lump. With the earpiece back in his ear, he adjusted the induction microphone and pressed the standby button.

"Sorry about that," he said under his breath, knowing the small microphone under his jaw would pick up the vibrations.

"Piccadilly line to Holborn Station, then change to the Central line."

Her response was terse, and he tried to break the tension. "It's a bit disturbing knowing you know where I am and where I am going before I do." There was no response. He knew he could turn off his phone, which would disable the GPS locator, but without her, he was lost. The escalator ended abruptly and he moved to the turnstiles, where he pulled his Oyster card from his back pocket. The reader accepted the payment, but he was not fast enough to see the charge and wondered how much credit was left on it. But like every other detail, he knew Alicia would take care of it. Aside from having to listen to her, she was very efficient.

The train arrived and Mako slid through the door, taking a seat when he probably should have displayed some chivalry and offered it to the harried woman dragging two kids behind her. Instead, he reached in his pocket for his phone and pulled up the Tube app. He studied the route and then opened the map app to get walking directions from Bank Station—something he should have done on an earlier scouting trip, but he had spent that time surveying the secretaries instead of the street signs.

Ten minutes later, he was shaken awake by the train stopping, and the recorded voice with a mediocre British accent reminded him to watch his step. Mako crossed to the Central line, leaned against a tiled wall and waited for the next train. Although the "G wagon" was now parked at Lloyd's of London, he was relaxed. It was not the SUV he was worried about, but rather the data its occupant was in the process of delivering. He would make his move when the transfer was done, preferably later that afternoon, when there would be little activity in the historic insurer's offices.

"Bank Station," Alicia said in his ear.

"As if I forgot," he muttered back and thought about turning her off. The hiss of the train's brakes announced its arrival before he saw it. It was Saturday and the train was quiet. He took an open seat for the five-minute ride. The train stopped and he exited at Bank, where he took the escalator two steps at a time, arriving quickly on the quiet street. With time to kill, he took Cornhill to Bishopsgate and turned into the Leadenhall Market, hoping to find an open pub.

The covered street was deserted, the Victorian-themed stores and bars closed for the weekend, and with regret he increased his pace and found himself staring at the "Death Star." The Lloyd's building, although not as well known as an architectural oddity like the "Shard," "Walkie-Talkie," "Cheese Grater," or "Gherkin," it deserved a nickname. The entire infrastructure was visible on the outside of the building—from glass-enclosed elevators to ductwork and plumbing pipes.

"Where is he?" he asked Alicia.

"Just pulled away. You should be clear now."

The connection had degraded. "What's up with the audio? We can't afford this now."

"*Afford* would be the critical word. We're out on a charter off West End in the Bahamas. Filling the tanks between dives."

He knew their financial situation was dire. Without this contract, he wasn't exactly sure what he would do. It wasn't like there was a heading for "spies wanted" in the classifieds.

"See what you can do. I really need you now." He was all

business, and with all his senses alert, he entered through the front door. The back door would be saved for his exit, once he had downloaded the data. Mako removed the fake ID card from his jacket pocket and placed the lanyard around his neck. With his head down, mimicking the posture of a defeated desk jockey forced to work on the weekend, he entered the building and presented the laminated card to an equally depressed security guard. They exchanged a look of brotherhood and he was waved in.

Where the building had its guts on display outside, the interior was sleek and modern. Mako went to the elevators and pressed the up button. The street grew smaller as he looked down through the glass enclosure, turning when the bell chimed indicating his floor. He exited and quickly moved to the perimeter of the mass of cubicles spread out in front of him. His six-foot frame was a detriment here, and he slouched as he moved to the back row. The doors around the perimeter leading to the managers' offices were closed, and he found a remote spot where he pushed the chair aside and kneeled down to conceal his head from view.

"Ready."

Alicia started to rattle off instructions, which he pecked onto the keyboard.

"Got it," she said.

He watched the screen as she had him enter seemingly meaningless lines of code.

"Put the drive in the USB port," she ordered.

"In," he said. The screen immediately changed to a status bar, and he watched as the files transferred. She had told him it was an encryption code. Lloyd's was always looking for new and innovative ways to stay in the spotlight of an otherwise mundane business. Over the years they had insured everything from Bruce Springsteen's voice to David Beckham's legs. Now they were moving to the world of data, hiring the best hackers to protect their systems. The status bar's progress slowed to a crawl at eighty percent. "This is really slow."

"That's why we have to do the transfer to the thumb drive. It has to be done on the property. Otherwise I could have done it myself."

Mako caught the barb, but ignored it. Alicia also had ties to the CIA. Once an employee, she was now working on a contract basis, as many of their old agents were. The new world of spying was now based entirely on speculation—fulfill the terms of the contract or no pay.

The elevator chimed and he glanced again at the status bar, now up to ninety-five percent. He lifted himself enough to peer over the top of the cubicle and saw several security guards exit the elevator, one going in each direction. Behind them was a dark-skinned man in a very expensive suit.

"I gotta go. They're on to us!" He forgot the bone mike and said the words out loud. One of the men's heads turned, and they started to weave through the aisle in his direction. "Now!"

"Two percent more," Alicia said calmly.

He willed the bar to one hundred percent and pulled the drive from the port. "Get me out of here."

CHAPTER 2

"Cody," Alicia called down to the deck of the fifty-two-foot sportfisher. She instructed Mako to stand by, took the headset off and handed it to Cody, her boyfriend, partner and captain, who had climbed the ladder to the flybridge. "He's all yours," she said calmly. It was not what she felt, but she trusted Cody's abilities to guide Mako out of the building, and she had to work on getting him out of the country. It would take both of them to salvage the operation. "GPS and autopilot are set." She grabbed her tablet and climbed down the stainless steel ladder to the gleaming white deck.

"Where's our first dive?" one of the men asked.

She thought for a minute. "Let's get you guys on the *Altar*. Nice coral heads and a ton of lobster."

The man glanced at his dive watch. "How deep for how long?" he asked.

Alicia was getting impatient. It wasn't the question—divers had been asking that since the birth of scuba. Their niche in a crowded market, although popular, was time-consuming, and time was one thing she didn't have right now. They had differentiated themselves from other charters by making aspects of technical diving available to the recreational diver on a live-aboard. This brought with it complicated machinery to fill the tanks as well as extra time supervising the divers. Enriched-air diving had gained in popularity, but was seldom offered on multi-day trips. The difficulty of mixing gases with the boat-mounted compressor had been overcome with Cody's mechanical skill and the computer interface she had designed to safely mix in the additional oxygen while mitigating the risks of explosion. They had developed their own system for overcoming the limiting factor in mixed-gas diving —depth. The standard mixes of thirty-two and thirty-six percent oxygen offered by dive shops limited divers to one hundred twelve and ninety-five feet respectively. With her algorithm, they custom-blended the gas for each dive. This allowed for deeper dives with maximum bottom time, but required expertise in mixing the gases.

"Everyone get suited up. We'll be on site in ten minutes." She had the group's attention now. "The *Altar* is in eighty-five feet of water, so we'll use a thirty-two percent mix. That should give you plenty of bottom time. Buddy up." The six charter customers went to their gear and started to prepare for the first dive of the day.

One of the women looked at her. "You're not going?"

"It's time to fly on your own. Stay with your buddies." Typically they waited until the final day of the charter before allowing an unsupervised dive, but this group had caught on quickly, and the dive was shallow enough to make the decompression stops minimal. She finished the briefing and watched while they checked the oxygen percentage in their tanks using the portable analyzer. She waited until they were in the water and each gave the OK sign before heading to the cabin, where she reached for the second headset. Cody, a master gamer, was in his element, guiding Mako to an air-conditioning vent to make his escape. Although Mako's life and their next boat payment were tied to the success of the operation, it was still a video game to Cody.

* * *

***

"Come on, Cody, there's no lock." Mako closed the door to the maintenance room and waited for his next instructions. He heard Cody humming in the background and looked around. A mop bucket and cleaning supplies were the only things present, and he doubted they would be any help. He was getting nervous, but had no choice but to trust the man on the other end.

"Look up. There should be a large vent cover. You'll need to open it and get inside," Cody said.

Hearing activity outside, he looked up as a last resort and saw the grille over his head. Without a choice, he grabbed the mop and smashed the handle into the grille. It didn't move. There were several voices outside now. He aimed for what he expected was a weak spot in the corner of the grate and with all his power pushed the handle through the gap. With a jerk, he pried the grille from the ceiling, ducking as it fell.

The door opened and he jumped. With the skill of a gymnast performing a muscle-up, he pulled himself through the opening, panicking for a second in the transition from the pull to the dip. A second later he was inside the duct, his arms trembling. The men were below him now, waiting as one talked into a microphone. His lanky frame and athletic ability had allowed him to enter the duct, and looking down on the guards, he risked a brief smile for they had neither the height or ability. They would need a ladder to follow. The Iranian came into the room, barked an order and left with one of the guards.

"You've got to climb the first ten feet. Then it'll level out and we can get you out of the building," Cody said.

Mako remembered the pipes running outside the tower and realized what Cody was up to. There was nothing to grab onto, so with his back to the duct, he pushed against the far side with his feet and inched upward. The bend that Cody told him about was visible a foot overhead, but just as he was about to enter the horizontal duct, he heard a rumble and was assaulted by a stream of air. It wasn't the pressure of the forced air but the dust it carried which caused him to sneeze and squint into the already-dark hole.

"Can you turn the damned thing off?" he asked Cody.

"Take too long. Gotta suck it up and get to level two."

Mako got the game reference and realized that things were not going to get any easier if he delayed. He lifted his body into the transition and crawled along the pipe. Suddenly the sound and vibration stopped and the air died, leaving his breath the only sound he could hear as it echoed off the steel duct. The pipe had transitioned from square to round, and he knew he was on the outside of the structure.

"What now?" he asked.

"Level five, dude. There'll be a service panel, but you'll have to slide down twenty feet. It gets easier after that. Once you're outside I'll send the elevator for you."

He couldn't help but hear the excitement in Cody's voice. This was like candy for the gamer. "Simple as that. Just send the elevator!" Mako reached another ninety-degree bend and braced himself for the fall. With his back to the duct, he started down. Leg shaking from the effort, he reached the next bend and looked around. "I'm not seeing it."

"Use your phone. It's there."

Mako took his phone from his pocket and turned on the flashlight. The bright light illuminated the duct, and just beyond his reach, across a larger duct, he saw the service door.

"Alicia, elevator to the sixteenth floor, please," he heard Cody say, relieved that they were both helping now.

"Just a second."

"I'm on the eighteenth floor!" Mako reminded them.

"Trust the Force," Cody replied.

"We have about an hour before the first diver is up," she said.

"A little help here," Mako responded, upset that he was not the center of their attention.

"As soon as you're on the elevator, I'll take you out," Alicia said.

Mako braced himself with his legs, extended his upper body over the void and grabbed one of the nuts holding the service door in place. He tried to turn it, but his hands were covered with sweat and he lost hold, almost dropping into the darkness below.

He reached back and dried his hand on his pants before grabbing the nut again. His grip was better, but it was too tight to loosen by hand. "I need tools." Remembering the shark-shaped key chain Alicia had given him, he withdrew it from his pocket and looked at the tiered shapes carved out of the interior. The void in the center of the tool fit over the nut, and he twisted it, using the teeth to grab the nut. With both hands on the tool, he turned it counterclockwise. It moved easily with the additional grip and leverage provided by the tool. He moved on to the next nut and quickly had all four off.

"Okay. What now?" he asked.

"There's a scaffolding running right outside. Push out the cover and you're out."

Mako turned off the light from the phone and placed it and the keychain back in his pocket. He eased himself forward and pushed against the door. It released and slammed onto the service scaffold fixed to the building. Light flooded the duct, and he breathed in the fresh air. Easing himself forward another few inches, he grabbed the edge of the opening and with a grunt pulled himself toward it. His fingers grabbed for the steel grating that made up the walkway for the scaffolding, but he didn't have enough momentum and his legs fell into the void, slamming against the duct as they hit.

He fought to pull himself up. Facing the duct, he reached the opening and worked his fingers forward an inch at a time, grabbing for another section of the open grate with each attempt. Finally he had enough leverage to pull himself through the opening, and his stomach dropped as he looked over the narrow scaffold at the street seventeen stories below. He waited, trying to control his breath, until he heard a motorized sound. He looked across at the exposed elevator shaft and crawled toward it, trying not to look down.

"The elevator is on its way. Climb on top and I'll take you down," Alicia said.

Mako waited for the elevator car to stop and crawled onto the elevator. Just as he braced himself, he felt his stomach drop again as it started to descend. It felt like the free-fall part of a sky dive and took him by surprise. Just as suddenly as it had started, the elevator slowed and stopped. He looked around before vaulting off and landing onto the hard sidewalk.

***

They heard the first diver at the swim platform and she checked her watch, surprised to see that an hour had passed. "Can you help the divers?" she asked Cody.

"Okay. I got it. You take Mako from here," he said.

"That'd be nice," Mako said. "I'm starting to feel a bit second-class here."

She ignored him and focused on her computer, logging out of the Lloyd's building site and hoping they insured themselves against computer fraud, because hacking in to their site had been all too easy.

"I'm still here," he said.

"Hold on." She pulled up the British Airways site and bought a one-way ticket from Heathrow to New York. The flight was scheduled to leave in several hours, so she was able to check him in and send the boarding pass directly to his phone.

"Flight leaves in three hours. Best bet is to backtrack to the tube station and ride out to Heathrow."

"Best check my Oyster pass too. Not sure what I've got on it."

Alicia opened another tab and went to the bookmark for the London Underground, where she added another twenty pounds to Mako's card. "Got it. You should be all set."

"A bit to eat would be nice. I'm a little low on cash, though."

She felt the boat shift from the weight of the divers. Ignoring the comment, she left the cabin and helped the excited divers aboard. She helped Cody release the spent tanks from the divers' backs and took their bulging catch bags full of lobster, which she placed in the cooler. Caught up in the divers' excitement, she forgot about Mako until she heard him in her ear.

"They're on to me. Going to need some help."

CHAPTER 3

The sidewalk was barren—no landscape, nothing to conceal him—so Mako did the only thing he could. He ran.

"I'm on the move," he said, hoping his words were intelligible over his ragged breathing. His legs still burned from climbing through the duct, but he fought through the pain. He had always been fast, and with a conscious effort to even out his breathing, he started to pace himself. But he was not fast enough. Every few seconds he turned to check on the men pursuing him and saw they were gaining. He had a block lead, enough to hide or change routes without them seeing, and regretted spending so much time researching the bars and pubs rather than devising an escape route.

"I need a plan," he said, gasping for air. There was nothing but static in his ear. "Come on, guys—a little help."

"On it." Cody's voice was hardly reassuring.

"Get me somewhere crowded. This business district is a ghost town." Mako backtracked to Leadenhall, doubting he could lose his pursuers there, but it was the only route he knew. "That market on the other side of the river. It's a madhouse."

"Got a name?"

"Borough Market," Alicia said. "And I'm guessing he didn't go for the food."

"Whatever," Mako said, struggling to talk and breathe at the same time.

"Okay. Zooming in now," Cody said. "Take care of the divers," Mako heard him say to Alicia. "I'll get him to Heathrow."

Mako looked behind him and saw the men closing. He picked up speed. When he reached the exit for the market, he took a guess and turned left, knowing the river was in that direction.

"You're on Gracechurch. In eight hundred feet, bear right onto King William. That will take you directly to London Bridge."

"Thank you, Siri," Mako said, knowing he should save his breath, but unable to hold the barb. He used the reflection from one of the store windows to check his pursuit and saw the Iranian still holding his pace, but the security guards had either gone back or fallen too far behind to matter. It was a one-on-one race. Increasing his speed again, he followed the bend in the road around to King William Street. The bridge lay ahead, a product of the seventies: low and architecturally insignificant, especially compared to the Tower Bridge on his left and the Millennium Bridge, visible in the distance on his right. He was running on fumes now, regretting that most of his efforts at the gym were spent in front of a mirror, working to keep his abs flat.

"The bridge is dead ahead," Cody said.

"Really. I hadn't noticed." Mako cursed under his breath and increased the length of his strides, trying to distance himself from the Iranian before he ran into the foot traffic on the bridge. The man was still behind him, but they appeared to be evenly matched. As long as he could maintain this pace until he reached the market, he knew he could lose him in its twisted alleys and throngs of shoppers. He crossed Lower Thames and in a dozen strides was on the bridge, where he was forced to slow to a fast walk as he weaved through the other pedestrians.

Thankful for the slower pace, he ignored the looks of the angry tourists he jostled as he moved by them. He chanced a second to look back. The man was still there and had somehow gained on him. Mako guessed he was leaving a path through the crowd, making it easy for the man to follow, but there was nothing he could do about it. Halfway across, he turned and saw the angry face of the Iranian only several bodies behind him. A stroller blocked Mako's path and he tried to push it out of the way until a rather large man turned and grabbed him.

The Iranian was standing right behind the irate father now, a sly grin on his face, obviously hoping he would do his work for him, but the man shoved Mako against the railing and moved away. With his back to the rail, Mako stared into the dark eyes of his pursuer. He looked right and left, realizing there was no way out. He would have to fight the man. He reached into his pocket for a pen, the closest thing to a weapon he carried. The flash of a knife blade caught his eye, and the man moved closer, the crowd parting as he stood only a foot away now.

Mako had his back against the low concrete wall that served as a railing. There was nowhere to go except over. He set his hands on the smooth top and vaulted to a catlike position on its flat surface. The hesitation cost him, allowing the man to lunge forward and catch him with the knife. Its razor-sharp blade penetrated his pants leg, tearing the fabric near the pocket and entering near his groin.

He felt the burn and knew he was bleeding but ignored the wound and looked down at the river. The water was gone, blocked by a large sightseeing barge filled with tourists all pointing up at him. The boat was moving, but he suspected the pilot had slowed to allow his passengers a better show than the Tower Bridge ahead.

Fortunately, it was high tide. Mako took the opportunity and jumped, landing on two tourists not fast enough to move out of his way. Screams came from the crowd as the barge picked up speed, the captain unaware of his new passenger. The crowd moved back, allowing Mako enough room to stand. Blood was trickling down his leg, but he guessed it was not a fatal wound and moved to the rail, checking himself for other injuries as he went. His hand reached down to the torn pocket and he realized the drive was gone.

Before he could react, he noticed a woman brave the gap between him and the crowd and approach.

"You're hurt," she said, with her hands out in front of her in a nonthreatening position. "I'm a doctor. Mind if I have a look?"

He looked down at his leg and noticed a small pool of blood on the deck. Nodding for her to approach, he looked ahead to see the barge moving towards a pier. "Hurry, though, I'll be needing to disembark." Something felt different when he spoke and he noticed the microphone was gone. Moving toward the crowd, he pushed aside several passengers and started searching the deck where he had landed. He felt the earwig still in place, but without the microphone it was little use. The woman touched him and he turned to her.

"Lie down," she said in an authoritative voice.

Exhausted and defeated, he sat on the deck with his legs in front of him. She knelt next to him, and he couldn't help but notice her scent as she leaned close and pulled the torn fabric away from the wound.

"I'd think a couple of stitches should do it," she said with an American accent. "Stay here, I'll see if they have a first-aid kit aboard." She got up and moved away.

The crowd was getting braver now, and he felt cornered. The woman approached, carrying a white box with a red cross on it. He was about to say he was okay, when the barge lurched forward. His immediate reaction was to run, but he quickly realized they had hit the dock. Two crewmen were running fore and aft with lines. He watched as both jumped on the dock at the same time and skillfully tied the barge off. The passengers, just a moment ago mesmerized by him, were now excitedly moving toward the starboard rail, pressing against each other, ready for their next adventure. He looked back and saw the woman still there.

"Might as well let me bandage you. It'll be a few minutes before they're off."

He nodded to her, but kept his eyes on the street above the covered walkway for any sign of police. The deck was almost clear when she finished. For the first time, he looked at her face and realized how pretty she was. He fought back against his natural reaction, knowing he had a flight to catch and no time for a dalliance. Instead of flirting, he merely thanked her.

She rejoined her friends waiting on the pier, and he followed, using them for cover as he climbed off the barge onto the dock. The women moved off to the right and he followed, staying far enough behind so they wouldn't feel him behind them. With every step he felt more secure, but the loss of the drive was now heavy on his mind. He left the main street and stepped into an alley, where he patted his good pocket and withdrew the phone, hoping it had not been damaged in the chase. The screen lit up, showing several text messages from Alicia. He texted his current situation, omitting the loss of the drive, and opened the map app. It showed him just a few blocks from the market. Quickly he cleaned himself off, arranging his shirttail to cover the rip in his pants. Keeping to the alleys rather than the main streets, he reached the market a few minutes later, his mouth watering at the sight of the food displays. He realized he hadn't eaten in hours and looked hungrily at the huge stacks of meat and cheeses.

His phone vibrated, distracting him from the gastronomic wonders, and he scrolled through Alicia's directions to the airport. After replying that he had received them, he checked his email, finding the receipt where she had added money to his Oyster card and another message with a PDF of his boarding pass to New York. He checked the time on the home screen and realized he had only two hours to make the flight.

Reaching into his back pocket, he was relieved to find his wallet still intact and withdrew a few notes. From the first stand he came across, he grabbed a few samples of cheese and waited for the man behind the table stacked high with food to acknowledge him. With a small loaf of bread and hunk of cheese in hand, he scanned the crowd for any sign of recognition. Finding none, he backtracked to the London Bridge.

An hour later, his stomach was full, but the desperate feeling of failure dominated his thoughts. He felt almost naked standing in front of the security guard at Heathrow. But with no baggage, he was quickly through security, and found his zone boarding when he reached the gate. After a quick moment of anxiety, he held his phone to the scanner. Relieved when it beeped and showed a green light, he walked down the jetway and smiled at the flight attendant who stood in the doorway directing passengers to their seats. He showed her his phone and she directed him to the far aisle, not failing to notice the smile and her touch as she directed him to his seat.

Settled back in the faux leather seat, his knees bumping the back of the seat in front, he stared at the screen of his phone and started typing the bad news. He reread the message several times before hitting the send button just as the plane was pushed back from the gate. Without waiting for the reply, he shut the power off and closed his eyes, wondering how he would overcome the setback. The loss of the drive and the bounty from the CIA would cost them, especially when Alicia saw the expenses he had incurred. With five hours to think about it, he tried to shut off his mind as the plane taxied. Half an hour later, they were still sitting on the runway, and he felt a hand on his arm. Opening his eyes, about to get angry with whoever was disturbing him, he quickly changed his attitude when he saw the flight attendant smiling at him.

"It's your leg, sir," she said. "Maybe we should have a look when we get airborne."

Mako looked down at the soaked bandage and up at the smile on her face, wondering if that was all she wanted a look at.

CHAPTER 4

Mako was getting impatient. The wait was interminable as the plane sat on the runway, waiting for some unspecified maintenance issue. The wound hurt and needed to be rebandaged. The flight attendant who had seemed so interested before was now ignoring him, having to answer questions from the other passengers about the delay. Finally, the pilot came over the intercom. Instead of an update, he started talking about finding your inner traveler, preaching to the restless passengers that they should remain calm and untroubled; that the delay was out of their hands, and getting anxious about connecting flights was not going to help. It didn't work on the other passengers and only aggravated Mako further as he fidgeted in his seat. He needed to use the bathroom, but he felt the jerk of the plane as it moved and the flight attendant advised him in a formal voice that no one could leave their seats until after they had reached cruising altitude. They were already over an hour on the ground, sitting in the sweltering heat, disconnected from the generator that ran the air-conditioning.

Finally they were airborne, and he relaxed slightly. The pilot announced that the universe was back in alignment, and Mako decided that was good enough to leave his seat. Excusing himself, he brushed by the woman next to him, who gave him a fake smile.

Uncertain if she saw the blood dripping down his side or if he had just upset her knitting, he slid past her and locked himself in the restroom.

After relieving himself, which took an inordinate amount of time in the shaking compartment, Mako removed his pants and sat on the toilet. The bandage stuck to the wound when he tore it off, but that was a good sign that the bleeding was stopping. Enough tissue was exposed that he suspected stitches would be in order, something he loathed. He looked around for anything to bind the wound for the five-hour flight when there was a knock on the door.

"Are you all right?"

He recognized the voice of the flight attendant and smiled. "I could use some assistance," he said and opened the bolt on the door. She slid in the narrow opening, and they stood with their bodies pressing together in the narrow space.

"That looks bad," she said and moved away for a better look.

"It'll keep until New York. I just need to stop the bleeding."

"How did you do it?" she asked.

Mako thought for a second about whether he should concoct a story, but decided on a different course. "Do you have a layover? It's a bit of a long story."

She ignored the question, smiled and removed a paper-wrapped cylinder from her pocket. At first he wasn't sure what she was doing, then he realized it was a tampon.

"This'll stop the bleeding," she said and placed it in the gash.

Her touch reached up to his groin and elicited a different response than she was looking for. She removed a roll of gauze and bound the tampon in place, then looked up at him and did what she could to put his world into alignment.

Maybe the pilot was right, he thought as he climbed over the knitting lady and took his seat. Minutes later, a smile on his face, he fell asleep.

***

"Call them back!" Alicia yelled to the bridge.

Cody hit the underwater horn three time, the prearranged signal for the divers to return to the boat. "What's up?" he called down to the deck.

"Weather coming." Several small anvil-shaped clouds had been on the horizon for an hour now. None big enough in itself to cause them any problem, but in the last half hour they had melded together into a massive single cell which was converging on the boat. With such a large storm threatening, bobbing around this close to the Gulfstream with divers in the water was not a safe situation.

Cody looked down at the indistinct mass of bubbles in the water. A storm could easily kick up the seas and put the divers in danger.

Alicia looked back at her screen after hearing the horn. Things were going from bad to worse—first the weather and now the news from Mako that the drive was lost. She quickly texted him back asking for more details, but figured it would be hours before she heard back from him. With her head in her hands, she sat on the bench the divers used to suit up. After a few deep breaths, she went back inside. It would take the divers at least five minutes to react and another three minutes to do the mandatory safety stop she had prescribed at fifteen feet. On her laptop, she opened a new window, where she logged into a private chat with her contact at the CIA. This was not going to be a conversation she wanted to have. Even though the coldness of the Internet connection would screen her from his wrath, she knew it would be there. But that was only part of it. She and Cody had invested most of their meager savings into this venture. The charter and dive business paid the bills, but it was more a lifestyle choice than a retirement plan.

She started typing as soon as the connection opened, explaining the circumstances that had led to the drive being lost. She heard activity outside the cabin and the distinctive sound of a large man stepping from the ladder to the deck. The divers were coming up, but Cody could handle them. She turned her attention back to the screen as letters appeared one by one. The secure interface had the feel of a 1980s computer game, and she had to wait as each word formed. The reprisal was instantaneous and condemned their actions, despite the fact that they were working on contract and would not get paid unless they produced.

The tirade over, she waited a few minutes and pasted in the reply that she had already composed. There had been no question how this conversation would go, and she'd wanted to be prepared with a well thought-out response. A favorable response appeared on the screen, but the last line shook her. "The Agency has decided that with another contractor involved, the chances for success are greater." She cursed under her breath—their exclusive contract was now open. Competition among contractors was often fierce, and this time, knowing the man she expected they would involve, it would be bad.

The bang of empty cylinders from the returning divers permeated the cabin. She shut down the chat screen and closed the cover on the computer. On her way out the cabin door to help Cody, she wondered if John Storm was just opening his computer now to find out the contract was open.

* * *

***

Foggy Bottom was suffocating. The late-June heat wave that had settled over Washington, D.C., made the city miserable, but was even worse in the low-lying areas built on filled-in swampland. The view of the Potomac was distorted by a layer of haze that had settled over the city. The vibration of the cell phone interrupted his thoughts as it echoed through the metal cafe table that just fit the confines of the small balcony. John Storm set down the newspaper. He regretted the adoption of the device, much preferring to go old school, but the darned things were too useful to ignore. His world had been a better place before the instant connectivity of the Internet and Wi-Fi. There was a time when people used to think about what they did and said before they broadcast it to the world. With a pained look, he picked up the phone.

The Facebook message looked innocuous on its own, but he knew different. John slid open the patio door and cringed at the blast of cool air that met him. Air-conditioning was a necessary evil here, and although he loathed it, everything he owned, especially his book collection, would be destroyed by the humid D.C. air without mechanical intervention. He sat at the desk and tapped the space button on his hardwired computer. He didn't trust Wi-Fi after watching a group of teenage hackers demonstrate to the Agency how easy the signals were to steal from the air. The wire offered him some comfort, but face-to-face was his preferred means of communication.

While the computer rebooted, he rose and went to the kitchen. Experience had also taught him that answering too quickly would only raise the price of the information. He pushed aside the espresso machine his daughter had bought him in another attempt at refinement, and pulled the old drip coffeemaker from the corner. Storm stood at the counter thinking about the message and watching the dark brew drip through the filter. He had grown restless between assignments, and he felt the familiar surge of adrenaline at the prospect of a challenge.

Five minutes later, with a hot mug of Folgers in hand, he sat down at the desk, logged in and smiled when he saw the message. It looked like Alicia and Mako had failed. He had been furious when they had been awarded the contract instead of him. *The Art of War* had instructed him to know his enemy, advice which he took to heart, and he had used all his contacts at the Agency to find out who had been awarded the contract. Now, the information was about to pay off. The Iranian was an old adversary, one he knew well from the days when subterfuge was more of a gentleman's game. But the playing field had changed, with technology supplanting tradecraft. The cubicle dwellers now had an advantage. Contracts were fewer and further between now, and he had to take whatever scraps were tossed his way.

He logged off and took his coffee and a legal pad back outside and started to plan. The first step was to find the Iranian. He started writing down a list of all the places he had encountered him over the years. London would not be safe for him after the failed attempt by Mako. It was well known that the Iranian loved his toys, and Storm thought for a minute before deciding the yacht would be his likely escape route. The ostentatious yacht christened *Shahansha*, the Persian translation for King of Kings, the title taken by Cyrus the Great, was large enough to sail anywhere in the world. It was a simple matter to find the ship's current location. He went back inside and opened the old version of Foxfire. The antiquated browser was slow and lacked bells and whistles, but it allowed him to disable all the tracking features hidden in the newer versions.

In the search window at marinetraffic.com, he entered *Shahansha* and waited. A tiny purple icon appeared and he zoomed in to its location. This might be easier than he'd thought.

***

Alicia removed the fill hose from the last tank and shut off the air compressor. The divers were asking questions about the next dive, which she answered abruptly. What had originally looked like a lifestyle job, running dive charters to exotic locations, was now interfering with her real work. She secured the fill hoses, closed the lid on the air station and climbed the ladder to the bridge, ignoring as many questions as she could.

Cody held his phone in landscape mode. "Stop with the games," she scolded him.

"Just killing time. Let them get a nice surface interval in before the next dive." He didn't look up from the screen.

She watched his hands work simultaneously and wondered how she could apply his gaming skills to the real world—to make some real money. "The contract's open," she said and laid out the details.

"Storm? Really?" he asked, finally looking up at her. "That dude's older than Pac-Man."

"He knows the target well. He's the logical choice."

Cody was silent for a minute. "Doesn't matter who it is. We have to save this deal or we lose the boat."

She placed a hand on his shoulder. "We'll get it, but I need a land-based Internet connection. The cell connection out here is too slow." She tried to reassure him, feeling guilty at the same time for placing him in this position. The dive shop he owned in Key Largo had provided an easy life and plenty of time for gaming, but that had all changed the moment Alan Trufante had introduced them. She had been an analyst with the Agency then, forced from her desk job into her first field work by a corrupt agent. She'd found herself in an unlikely alliance with Mac Travis and his troublesome sidekick. Now Cody was in danger of losing everything he had, and it was her fault.

"We can see what this storm does. Use it as an excuse to pull the plug and head into West End," he said.

She thought for a minute, trying to balance their priorities. Whatever happened with the contract, they still needed to keep this a viable business, and with Internet reviews ranking on the first page of Google, they couldn't afford any bad press. "Let's drop them on the wall for a deep dive and then do a quickie on the reef." She looked at the dark clouds on the horizon.

Cody followed her eyes. "It's moving to the west. If we head east, we should miss it entirely." He started the engines. "You up for a dive? I'm not feeling good about dropping them on the wall without someone to keep an eye on the max depth. Give them a twenty-eight percent mix. That'll get them to one hundred thirty feet and keep the bottom time short."

The wall he referred to was exactly that, a sheer face of coral dropping deep to the ocean floor. It took an experienced diver to maintain depth in the clear water, where depth perception was almost impossible. It would be her job to stay at the maximum depth, giving the divers a reference to stay above. "It'll give me a chance to think," she said and climbed down the ladder.

CHAPTER 5

Alicia was the last in the water. She strapped into her equipment and slid to the end of the bench, where she put on her fins and mask. Before she got up, she placed the regulator in her mouth and started breathing. The transom door was only two feet away, an option she insisted on. Typically installed for hauling large fish onto the boat, with the added swim platform, it made getting in and out of the water easier, not only for her, but for their clients. She stood, bracing herself as her body took the weight of the tank, and shuffled her fins through the door and onto the platform. With one hand on her mask and the other over the regulator, she took a giant stride and jumped.

The water was brilliant, the shelf where the reef dropped off to the abyss clearly visible almost eighty feet below. This time of year, her shorty wetsuit was warm now, but she knew in forty minutes, when she planned to surface, it would be needed.

She followed the divers down the anchor line, taking her time to clear her ears as she descended. The group met at the anchor, where she made eye contact and gave the OK signal to each diver, checking their expressions as they signaled back. She was looking for signs of fear and anxiety, something she would keep in mind along the way. Once everyone had acknowledged her, she finned off in the direction of the wall.

The coral heads and soft sponges prevalent on top of the reef disappeared as she crossed over the void. Despite the hundred-foot-plus visibility, when she looked down, the water faded slowly to black, the bottom a thousand feet below. Slowly she led the group down to a hundred feet, watching them carefully for signs of nitrogen narcosis. She checked her stopwatch and dive computer. They were already almost ten minutes into the forty-minute dive profile. The computer was set for the custom Nitrox mix strapped to her back, and showed a longer no-decompression time than the profile she had assigned the other divers, but with a group they would need to stay together. When the watch hit twenty minutes, she would turn and start back.

The hundred-and-thirty-foot depth, the limit for recreational divers, was like a magical number for intermediate divers. It was not a big difference, but diving walls was more dangerous than a reef. With the clear water and no references, it was hard to maintain a consistent depth. Personally, she didn't get the allure of deep diving. There were some neat things not seen shallower, but the increased air consumption and decreased bottom time made shallower diving more appealing.

With her LED light, she scanned the crevices in the coral, pointing out anything unique or interesting to the group. Several eels popped their heads out, but pulled back into their holes when the divers approached. She got excited when a large eagle ray appeared below them, gliding effortlessly with the current.

She glanced at her watch, realizing that they were at the turnaround time, and with a tap of her finger on her outstretched palm asked them to signal how much air they had left. One of the women seemed distracted and disoriented. She motioned the group ahead and went to check on her. Alicia tapped the woman on the shoulder and immediately saw the fear in her eyes. Her tank valve bumped a coral head when she turned, and her eyes widened further. Alicia moved closer and reached for the diver's air gauge. The needle was already in the red, showing only five hundred PSI remaining. Most divers were instructed to plan on being back at the boat with that much air. In her present condition, the woman would not make it back at all. Alicia automatically reached for the alternate air source clipped to the right side of her BC and released the clip.

Before handing the regulator, known as an octopus, to the woman, she checked her own gauges. With over two thousand PSI, she had more than half a tank and decided it would be better to buddy-breathe back to the boat. That would leave the other woman with at least some air in her tank if something happened. She handed the yellow regulator to the woman, who gave her a questioning look, and Alicia realized how bad this could get.

The woman pushed away the regulator and continued to stare at the wall. Alicia had to take matters into her own hands now and calculated how long their combined air supply would last. Math was difficult at this depth, and she was working through the numbers when a turtle floated below them. Suddenly, the woman tore away, finning frantically to catch it. Alicia followed in her bubble trail, very conscious that she was exceeding the maximum depth for the gas mix, but also knowing there was a safety factor that equated to about fifteen feet built in.

She kicked down to the woman, who had lost the turtle and was looking around, flapping her hands. She might not leave a good review on the Internet, but a bad review was better than a dead client, Alicia thought as she grabbed her tank valve.

This part was all theory. She had gone through the diver training quickly, easily satisfying her instructors, but had never performed a real-life rescue. The woman flailed, not understanding what was happening. Alicia inflated her BC, using the added buoyancy to bring them higher in the water column. When they reached the reef, she released the signal buoy clipped to her side. The idea was to mark their position, get to the surface and let Cody come to them.

She opened the buoy, pulled the regulator from her mouth and pressed the purge valve. A burst of air shot from the regulator into the air chamber of the marker, causing the red tube to rise. She was about to follow behind it when she realized the woman was no longer by her side. She looked down and saw her stuck under an outcropping, her regulator hanging free in the water.

***

John Storm waited at the ticket counter, getting impatient with the family ahead of him. He checked his watch again—twenty minutes to board—and tried to catch the agent's eye. The kids were playing with the stanchion marking the end of the line, taking the ribbon off and running in circles with it. His eyes bored into the back of the incompetent father's head in frustration, and he was about to do something he would regret when the agent handed the man back his credit card. He breathed deeply, but instead of putting his wallet away, the man removed another card and handed it to her.

The kids were screaming now, their parents ignoring them, when another agent finally appeared and motioned John to the counter. He gave her the flight information and asked for a one-way ticket, for which he would pay cash.

If it were a bank teller, she would have pushed the alarm button. The perfect profile of a terrorist stood in front of her. He gave her a reassuring look, having been in this situation many times, choosing the ridicule and the extra attention he would receive at security for the anonymity of paying cash. He looked at his watch again when finally she handed him his change and boarding pass.

Security was thorough, but with only a small carry-on, he suffered the scrutiny, laughing to himself at the inadequacy of their procedures. If he wanted to get something past them, and many times he had, it would be a simple matter. TSA agents checked what you packed—not what you packed it in. There were all manner of ways to disguise objects in the hardware of a travel case.

He walked swiftly to the gate, where the agent gave him a hurried look as she took his pass and closed the door behind him. He entered the jetway and made his way to his seat. The last-minute booking resulted in a middle seat, and he settled in for the flight to San Juan, where he would catch a puddle jumper to Virgin Gorda.

***

Mako walked off the plane feeling better than he deserved. After the rendezvous with the flight attendant, he had slept the entire flight. It always amazed him how the world didn't look so grim after some sleep. He was confident that, with Alicia's help, they would find another way to get the data on the lost drive.

He waited by the gate for the flight attendants to finish their closeout procedure and exit the plane. Standing by the ticket counter, he texted Alicia, asking for any information and hoping he would have the night in New York with the blonde, who smiled when she exited the jetway. She said something to the other attendants and walked over.

"A little close quarters for a proper invitation in there." He smiled. "But if you're open, I could buy you dinner."

"I've got an early flight tomorrow," she said.

Unsure if she was begging off or just making him work harder, he countered, "We can make it early to bed, then."

She hooked her arm in his. "If you understand those are the rules," she said.

On the way to the exit, he used his phone to hook up with an Uber driver. They bypassed the waiting cabs and hopped into the Pathfinder. "West Eighty-Second, by…," he told the driver.

"It's on the app. Got it," the driver said.

"Nice neighborhood." She smiled.

"Chinese?" he asked and reached for his phone, both to check if Alicia had answered and to order food.

"That'd be great," she said and slid closer.

He finished ordering and gave the driver the address for the restaurant.

***

It would have been better if the diver was unconscious, Alicia thought as she released air from her BC and descended to the woman struggling to remove her arm from the coral head. The question of what it was doing there and how it had gotten stuck flashed through her mind, but she put it aside for later. As disoriented as the woman was, anything could have happened.

Once she had reached the Rescue Diver level, her instructors had started to tell the stories of their favorite FUBARs—*f'ed up beyond all recognition.*

Alicia swept her right arm around her side, recovered the octopus and, instead of handing it to the woman, reached out and stuck it into her mouth. The panic in her eyes subsided briefly as she quickly inhaled. Alicia didn't bother to check her gauges. During her training, several dives had been designed for her to run out of air; to learn the feeling of sucking on a near-empty tank and how many breaths to expect once it started. She would know when to take the last breath and head for the surface, hopefully with the woman in tow.

The line from the buoy was in her way when she reached around to free the woman. Unclipping it from her BC, she attached it to the woman, trying not to think that she might be marking the body. A green ooze floated from the coral head as Alicia tried to extract the woman's arm. The hold seemed to tighten like a Chinese puzzle; the more she pulled, the firmer the grasp of the coral.

She checked her air and, with only five hundred PSI remaining, reviewed her options. The best solution was to leave the tank with the woman, surface and return with tools and two fresh tanks. A quick glance at her watch showed they were well past the no-decompression limit. They would have to deal with that issue after they had the woman on the surface. Alicia unbuckled her BC and left it next to the woman. She gave her a reassuring look and took a long breath, removed the regulator and finned for the surface. The visibility made the ascent appear easier than it was, and it took her last gasp or air to reach the surface. The buoy floated next to her, but the boat was still anchored several hundred yards away.

Without the aid of her BC, she had to tread water to stay above the surface. With the buoy in her hand to prevent the current from taking her, she screamed for Cody. Whitecaps covered the surface, brought by the leading edge of the storm. The seas were not dangerous to dive in under normal circumstances, but they seemed huge as she fought to keep her head above water. There was no answer from the boat and she started to panic. The woman didn't have enough air for the time it would take her to swim to the boat —in fact, she might be out now. She pushed that thought from her mind and screamed louder. They had to be looking for her. She was well past her dive profile, and the other divers should have reported the situation to Cody. Finally she heard someone call out from the boat and the engine start. The sound of the windlass pulling the anchor chain carried clearly across the water, and within a few minutes, Cody skillfully placed the stern of the boat by her.

"Get me a BC and two air tanks!" she called from the water. Treading water, even with the fins, was taking a toll on her, and she worried about the increased bottom time, but she was already in the water. She could take the tank down and resurface. "Get Cody in the water with me," she called to the closest diver. "And tell him to bring a pry bar." He had the experience to deal with the situation below and had not been in the water today. The other divers would be in danger of decompression sickness if they returned to depth this quickly.

She inflated the BC and flipped it over her back. The second tank, a smaller pony tank about a quarter the size of a regular tank, was handed to her, and she descended. The extra weight of the second tank took her quickly to the bottom, but hindered her as she made her way back to the woman. Fortunately, a small stream of bubbles rose above her, indicating she was still breathing. Once there, Alicia replaced the near-empty tank with the pony bottle and gave her the OK sign. A figure in the water above made her jump, but she relaxed when Cody appeared next to her. He gave her the thumbs-up sign that she should ascend and leave him with the woman.

The fresh tank gave her plenty of air for a long decompression stop. At thirty feet, her computer beeped, indicating a stop of five minutes. She adjusted the air in her BC to keep herself in place and waited. She was close enough to the bottom to see the two figures below, but there was little detail. Cody appeared to be working to free her, but after her five-minute stop, she lost sight of them as the dive computer updated itself, indicating that she needed to move up the water column to fifteen feet, where she would remain for ten minutes. While she waited, she started to calculate the woman's situation. Alicia's watch showed she had been in the water for over an hour. That would place the woman below in severe danger of decompression sickness.

With two minutes left in her safety stop, she saw action below her. The two figures rose to the surface and stopped below her. Cody held the woman with one hand and adjusted both their BCs with the other. For now, they were doing the right thing. Alicia's time was up, and she added a blast of air to the BC and surfaced. The other divers helped her out of the water, and she gave several orders while she slid onto the bench, clipped the tank onto the rack behind her and slithered out of the gear. One of the men threw a line with a dive weight tied to the end behind the boat and tied it to a nearby cleat. With this, Cody could hold onto the line, making the safety stops easier.

CHAPTER 6

Mako's third-floor walk-up above a busy restaurant was a single room with a closet-sized kitchen and an even smaller bathroom, but it was all he could afford. The woman snoring quietly next to him had not seemed to notice and was more impressed by the address than the surroundings. The night had been a good one. Mako rolled out of bed and looked over at the body beside him, hesitant to leave. But he was anxious to see if Alicia had left instructions. He got up and went to the kitchen, where he started coffee. The sky was just starting to lighten when the water boiled, and he poured it into the French press. While he waited for it to brew, he checked his phone to see if Alicia had called or texted overnight. There was nothing, and he wondered why she hadn't given him directions. The mission was time-sensitive, and even wasting the night, as pleasurable as it was, might cost them the contract.

The sound of bare feet coming from the next room brought his attention back to the present. He watched the flight attendant head to the bathroom, flashing him a shy smile as she passed the small kitchen. The brew looked to be dark enough, and he carefully applied pressure to the handle, forcing the screen to push the grounds to the bottom of the glass decanter. Sitting back, he sipped his coffee while he watched her get ready, and a few minutes later, with a quick peck on the cheek, she was gone.

Mako was anxious and decided to go for a run. He dressed and headed down the three flights of stairs, pausing in front of the restaurant to stretch before starting at a slow pace toward Central Park. With every step, he felt the gash in his thigh, but after being run down in London, he was dedicated to improving his fitness—at least for today. This early, the city was quieter than one might expect. Manhattan started late and ended late. He headed up Eighty-First, crossed Central Park West and picked up his pace as he joined the trail. A few other joggers, mostly women, made eye contact, but for the most part, he was caught up in his own thoughts, wondering what happened to Alicia and where he would go next. Five miles and forty-five minutes later, he was back in front of the restaurant, checking out the pastries in the window. His breathing back to normal, he walked up the three flights to his apartment. Standing in the small kitchen, he filled a glass with water, took several long sips and gobbled down the pastry he had just bought, letting the crumbs fall in the sink. He refilled the glass, sat down and checked his phone again. There was still nothing from Alicia, and not wanting to wait any longer, he pecked out a message to her.

***

Alicia woke the next morning wondering where she was. Exhausted when they'd finally docked late last night, she had decided the woman's life was more important than the contract and stayed with her until they had both fallen asleep. She had no idea how she had reached their berth. Finally her tired brain pieced all the clues together; they were docked in the marina at West End on Grand Bahama Island. Typically, to give a more adventurous feel to the trip and avoid the cost, they anchored over a shallow reef, in easy snorkel reach of the abundant lobster and conch. Unless forced in by bad weather, they never docked. This time was different. They had wanted to make sure the woman got medical attention if she needed it, and the marina's Internet connection should be fast enough for her to do her work. Unless the marina was busy, which usually only happened during fishing tournaments, there would be plenty of broadband for what she needed.

The boat was quiet, the divers probably sleeping after the late night fueled by rum drinks from the tiki bar and the excitement of the rescue yesterday. It was dark by the time they had completed the decompression stops needed for the woman and gotten her onboard. The other divers had been great, willing to take turns keeping her company in the water as she waited for the nitrogen to leave her blood. Fortunately her wrist and arm were just scraped, nothing deep enough to require medical attention. They would have to keep an eye on her, though. After that long in the water, there was still a chance of coming down with the bends, and coral cuts were often easily infected. She rolled over in the large forward V-berth, looking for Cody, but his space was empty and cold.

She got up, put on a t-shirt and shorts, and went up to the bridge, where she sat down next to Cody, taking his coffee and sipping it before they spoke. He had the look of someone who had been up all night, and he probably had.

"Where to?" he asked.

She placed her hand on his forearm, leaned over and kissed him, wondering again if she had ruined his life. After another sip of his coffee, she took the mug to refill it. "I need to get on the computer and figure some things out. Hopefully the Wi-Fi is fast enough."

"After yesterday, I think this whole group could use a break. I was planning to head back to the *Altar* and do the shark dive, but I'm thinking we should probably do something tamer. Maybe hit a couple of shallow reefs where they can get some good bottom time, hunt some lobsters and maybe shoot some fish."

"Sounds good." Alicia turned and went down the ladder. He was right. Taking home lobster or fish would take any sour taste from their mouths. She refilled Cody's mug and slipped carefully past the sleeping divers, grabbing her laptop on the way out of the cabin. After handing the coffee up to him, she stepped over the gunwale and onto the dock. A short walk to the end of the pier brought her to a coffee shop, where she ordered a latte and opened her laptop in a quiet corner. It didn't take her long to immerse herself in her trade. She methodically went from source to source, checking all the resources she had. Credit cards, airline flights, anything that would give her an indication where the Iranian had gone. The man was invisible, having the luxury of his own fleet of jets and boats. It wasn't lost on her that John Storm had resources beyond her reach and probably had a head start. It would be hard to trace him, but finally she saw one of his known aliases on a flight from Atlanta to San Juan. From there it was easy to find his reservation to Spanish Town in the British Virgin Islands. She leaned back and smiled for the first time in two days. Finding Storm would lead them to the Iranian.

Just as she closed her laptop, the message from Mako appeared on her phone. *Head to La Guardia*, she texted back, *and pack tropical. I'll load your flights into your phone shortly.* With the laptop under her arm and the unfinished coffee in her other hand, she headed back to the boat. The divers were starting to stir now, and she started breakfast. While the fresh lobster sautéed, she started to scan her phone for flights to Tortola. When the meat was translucent, she poured the egg mixture in and booked his flight to San Juan while the dish cooked. Once the divers were in the water, she could make the other arrangements and email Mako his boarding pass.

While the divers dug into the lobster-scrambled eggs, she went over to Cody, who was talking to the woman they had rescued yesterday. Without wanting to disturb them, she walked close enough to hear the conversation, making sure that the woman was okay before she interrupted. "How are you feeling?" she asked.

The woman looked up at her, clearly exhausted. "I don't think I'll be diving anymore today, but I don't want to ruin the charter for anyone else, so if you guys want to head out, that's fine with me. I'll just hang out on the boat."

Cody looked at Alicia. "We're due to head back tonight anyway. How about we go to the *ups and downs* and then do one last shallow drop. The forecast looks favorable to cross the Gulfstream this afternoon. We can be back by six or so."

The state of the Stream was always a concern on these trips, and Alicia relaxed a little knowing the crossing wouldn't be the bone-jarring slugfest it could be. Tonight she would be at home with full broadband access, able to steer Mako to the Iranian.

***

Cursing overnight travel, John Storm got off the plane and climbed down the ladder to the steamy tarmac. It was one thing getting to San Juan, but flights out were limited, and he had arrived too late for the Cape Air flight to the BVI. Congress had seen to it that there were no longer any guarantees or expense accounts in his business, and he slept in the terminal instead of booking a hotel. The first flight out was at eight a.m., and he sat behind the pilot, his favorite spot in a small plane, where he was able to watch the gauges and controls of the aircraft. It was a brief flight, less than an hour, mostly over water until St. John and St. Thomas appeared on the right. The pilot stayed seaward of the smaller islands and landed on the small airstrip in Spanish Town. Virgin Gorda's airport was smaller than Tortola across the channel, but closer to the Costa Smeralda Yacht Club, known locally as the YCCS, where the radar transponder had shown the Iranian's boat was docked.

After clearing customs and immigration, he found a pay phone and called the hotel at Leverick's Marina. It was as close as he could get to the YCCS. The more laid-back complex was affordable and had a great tiki bar. With his lodging handled, he found a cab and bartered with the driver for the cross-island drive. Leverick's was less than six miles away, but the drive would take close to an hour on the island's steep inclines and winding roads.

Feeling slightly ridiculous in the tourist wagon, a pink bus with exposed bench seating in the rear, he left the airport. Twice, the driver stopped on the descent from Gorda Peak to let the brakes cool down. Finally, tired and impatient, Storm was dropped off by a small grocery store. He paid the driver and wandered down the hill to the water. Bypassing the hotel office, he turned to the left and entered the shade of the bar. It was almost noon. He needed a drink and a plan.

The Dark and Stormy quenched his thirst and took the edge off his mood. The bartender came by to see about a refill, but he declined and paid. There was work to be done today if he wanted to stay ahead of Alicia and Mako. He slung the messenger bag over his shoulder and climbed the stairs that wound up the hill to the hotel, where he checked in to the cheapest room they had. The bed looked inviting, but it would have to wait. He changed clothes. Despite the heat and humidity, he opted for lightweight long pants and a long-sleeve shirt, knowing the mosquitos would be worse than the heat. With his field glasses around his neck, he left the room and locked the door, leaving a piece of his hair wedged in the jamb. It was an old trick, but would tell him if anyone entered when he was gone.

Descending the winding exterior stairway, he looked down at the busy marina. Several dive and fishing charter boats occupied the closest slips, then came the few private and charter sailboats, all with thick yellow cords hooked to the shore power. The additional forty-dollar charge for a slip instead of a mooring ball allowed the air-conditioners to run. He approached a small shack on the end of the dock, where a dark-skinned man in a tropical uniform nodded to him from a chair set in the shade.

"Afternoon, sir."

"Can you get me a water taxi over to the small restaurant past the yacht club?"

"Oh, the Fat Virgin." He nodded back and removed a VHF radio from a clip on his belt. A few minutes later, a yellow boat with a glass enclosure pulled alongside the dock and hovered without tying up. Storm boarded the taxi and sat in the seat to the side of the driver. Water gurgled behind the transom as the transmission slipped into gear and the boat moved forward. Thankfully, the old diesel inboard was too loud to comfortably talk over, allowing him to observe the shoreline in silence. He had seen no marked roads between Leverick's and the YCCS on a small tourist map, and now he studied the shoreline for any trails or private roads that might allow him access if he needed it. They passed a point and headed across the water, where the boat entered a narrow bay, the ocean visible across a thin land mass at the end. Storm was more interested in the long dock on the right. It was designed to be a statement and had achieved its goal. Several hundred feet of freshly painted deck, with shiny black pilings standing sentry every twenty feet. Just inside of the main pier were rows of slips, mostly empty except for the half dozen small yachts there. As impressive as the facility was, the two large boats tied up at the end made it look insignificant.

"It is the big money there," the driver said over the rumble of the motor, probably expecting John to be one of the gawking tourists that always urged him to get as close to the megayachts as he would allow.

John nodded back without taking his eyes off the compound.

A quarter mile past the resort, the pilot pulled up to a small dock.

Storm paid the driver and walked down the dock, found a small sidewalk and cut behind the kitchen of a small, colorful restaurant. The road which he had seen from the water looked like it led most of the way to the luxurious resort. As he approached, the hotel behind the docks came into view, its tower visible above the trees, and he moved to the shadows to avoid the guards he expected to be patrolling the perimeter. The resort was a step above exclusive, allowing no one but its guests access to the amenities—and he didn't look like a guest.

Storm checked the road, crossing where it ran by the docks. He settled into a clump of bushes and did his best to adjust his body for an extended stay. Thankful for his choice of attire, he tried to ignore the mosquitos and trained his binoculars on the yacht. From his vantage point, the names were hidden by the dock in front, but he knew the Iranian's vessel.

At eighty-five meters, over two hundred fifty feet long, the sleek yacht towered over the docks, her tower sitting over fifty feet above the water. He knew the specs and tried to look past the two nearly naked women sunbathing by the pool. The yacht was a statement, and at close to a hundred million dollars, it was the top tier of luxury. Three men sat around a table in the shade off to the side of the pool, but he couldn't see who they were until a crew member waiting on them moved. He clenched his jaw as the Iranian laughed.

CHAPTER 7

Mako studied the wound in the small bathroom. He winced when the tampon pulled free, but the bleeding had stopped, and only a few bright drops showed where the fabric had stuck. With a cotton ball soaked in hydrogen peroxide, he cleaned the gash and applied a new dressing. He took a half dozen steps to the tiny kitchen, brewed another pot of coffee and packed.

A few minutes later, he was in an Uber cab headed back to the airport. The driver was male and chatty, neither appealing to his social instincts, but the cars were cleaner than the city cabs and within his budget. And with the loss of the drive, money was quickly becoming an issue. Half an hour later, he stepped onto the curb at LaGuardia Airport and tipped the driver, the payment automatically coming from Alicia's account—just another reason to use the service.

The glass doors slid open and he entered the terminal. The continuous stream of people pushing bags and pulling children appeared daunting. Stepping into the flow of traffic reminded him of entering a busy freeway. Getting through security was a simple matter, especially with the TSA pre-check Alicia had arranged, and minutes later, he was sipping a glass of wine at the bar by the gate. It wasn't yet noon, but he knew he would need all the patience he had for the trip, first to San Juan and then the puddle jumper to Tortola.

The British Virgin Islands were not unfamiliar to him, but his memory of previous trips was clouded by alcohol. He would have to rely on Alicia to give him more specifics. The boarding process had just started when he texted her asking for more details. He boarded, groaning to himself about the middle seat. The plane pulled back from the gate, and the male flight attendant gave him a look as his phone chimed. He glared back, sneaked a peak at the screen and smiled. The easiest and least conspicuous way to get around the small chain of islands was in a sailboat, and she had rented him one. Many cruisers had little sailing skill and just motored around—with his limited boating abilities, he would fit right in.

The attendant gave him another look as the pilot taxied to the runway, and he finally shut off the phone, hoping there would be a better level of service on this flight than it appeared. Once the plane had reached cruising altitude, he pulled out his laptop and connected to the plane's Wi-Fi, not caring about the cost as again it went on Alicia's account. He studied a map of the islands, committing it to memory, and found the marina where the sailboat was reserved. It was a twenty-minute cab ride from the airport, and he tried to decide if he had enough time to stop for provisions on the way or wing it with the restaurants and boatside delivery services.

He was disappointed again as two men pushed the drink cart down the aisle and briskly asked for his drink order. Finally, with two empty Grey Goose vodka bottles in front of him, he closed his eyes and slept until the plane bumped to a stop in San Juan, Puerto Rico.

Expecting air-conditioning, he was surprised by the humidity as he entered the terminal. It looked like it had come out of a build-your-own-airport kit and assembled by someone who didn't know how to put the parts together. The walk to Cape Air took him through several different sections, each marked by a clear transition and different architectural style. After several long hallways, he found the small desk and checked in for the flight.

The crowd here was different, mostly tourists excited about their upcoming trip. As he approached the counter, he noticed an attractive woman in uniform pass by, slide a card into the lock and exit the terminal. He checked in and went to the window, where he watched her board the ten-seater, hoping the plane would be his. The agent at the desk called the flight, and he swiftly moved to the front of the line, wanting the copilot's seat. His phone vibrated and he checked the message while the agent checked boarding passes and passports. It was Alicia again, letting him know that Cyrus, the Iranian, was on Virgin Gorda. How she compiled her information was a constant mystery to him, but as a partner she was top-notch. The door opened and he was first into the heat, leading the group down the stairs and onto the hot tarmac.

At the boarding steps, he squeezed between a couple placing their bags on a cart next to the ladder and was first to climb the stairs. He looked into the cabin of the aircraft and smiled at the pilot. "This seat taken?"

She barely acknowledged him, but nodded it was okay, and he slid into the right-hand chair. While observing her as she went through the preflight checklist, he practiced his Sherlock Holmes, trying to put the pieces of her life together. First and most important, there was no ring. That hadn't stopped him before, but it did complicate things. Next he studied her face—she was striking, and he wondered what she would look like out of the standard-issue pilot's uniform. He could see curves, but the unflattering cut made them indistinct. She was tan, a good sign that she had enough time off to enjoy the outdoors.

He continued to observe, choosing to leave her to her work, but admiring the efficiency of her movements. She completed the checklist and looked back at the cabin, locking eyes with him briefly before focusing on the other passengers. After a quick welcome and safety briefing, she put on her headset and asked the tower for permission to take off. Unfortunately, there was no way to start a conversation with the large headphones she wore, and he tried to figure out a way to talk to her once they were in the air.

The plane revved and started down the runway, fishtailing as it picked up speed. The wheels left the ground, and Mako was pushed back in the seat from the slight G force of the takeoff. The pilot adjusted several controls, and he relaxed as the plane settled into its cruising altitude high above the deep blue water.

He was about to tap her on the shoulder when he noticed a headset hung from a small hook by his legs. She glanced at him and smiled when he put it over his ears, and the next thing he heard was her voice.

"Well, hello."

"Back at ya," he said, adjusting the volume knob on the right ear. "Didn't think I'd get a chance to say hi."

"Well, hi. Staying in Tortola long?" she asked.

"A little work—a little play. On a sailboat, though, so...." Air traffic control from St Thomas cut him off and she went back to work. The chatter was fairly constant for the next thirty minutes as she adjusted course, and he could see the islands ahead. St. Thomas handed her off to Tortola, who issued a course and altitude change, taking them over the pristine horseshoe-shaped coves of Jost Van Dyke. She banked and veered left, descending as they crossed the larger island of Tortola and landed.

"I love to sail," she said.

He thought for all of two seconds before responding. "And you are welcome aboard."

"I've only got two days," she said and cracked the door to let some fresh air in as they taxied.

"We'll just have to make the best of it." The list of things that could go wrong with this scenario was endless, but he put them to the back of his mind, deciding to rationalize it as "good cover."

Half an hour later, they had cleared the small customs line and went to a small shack across the street, where the taxi drivers were gathered in the shade, playing checkers and sipping cold drinks.

"Hillary, by the way," she said with some sort of a mild accent that he couldn't place—yet.

"Mako," he answered and formally extended his hand. She laughed and accepted it, twisting it slightly with a firm grip, giving a hint of what might be in store later.

It was almost four when they left the airport, endangering his plan to get out of the harbor tonight. There were several islands across the bay that had good anchorages and more privacy than the tourist-trodden docks of the marina. He decided to skip the grocery store and stop at the liquor store, where they carefully selected a few bottles of wine and a large bottle of rum, along with some chips and nuts. They arrived at the marina with one bag of provisions and checked in.

They were assigned a thirty-eight-footer and given directions to the slip. Pushing the cart containing little baggage and less provisions ahead of him, they greeted the other cruisers preparing to head out. Toward the end of "B" dock, they found the boat and laughed out loud at the name on the back: *Escape Yourself.*

They quickly unpacked and went on deck to wait for their briefing. Hillary had been here several times and went quickly through the rundown while Mako sat entranced by the melodic accent of the dark-skinned woman. Everything that came out of her mouth sounded like an exotic song. Finally he signed the papers, and she called for assistance to help them out of the tight slip. Several dockworkers came over, skillfully released the lines and wished them a good trip before they pushed the boat into the channel.

With the sun just starting to set behind them, he pushed down the throttle and steered through the buoys until they were in open water. With Hillary navigating, they left the protection of the bay and fought the afternoon swells driven by the tradewinds as they motored across the channel, heading for Cooper Island, where they planned to moor for the night.

It was near dark when he extended the boat hook over the bow and reached for the line attached to the mooring ball. Hillary ran a boat as well as a plane and judged the wind and currents perfectly. *Escape Yourself* coasted to a stop right at the ball, and he pulled the line aboard. She came forward and showed him how to loop the dock line through the eye in the mooring line and attach it to two cleats for a better hold, and he patted her bottom as she led the way back to the cabin.

Fifteen minutes later, they docked the dinghy at the Copper Island Beach Club and ordered Cooper Cules from the small walk-up bar. They took the drinks and selected a secluded spot amongst the comfortable chairs and couches which were scattered in several different seating arrangements. Sipping the cocktail made from muddled cucumber, lime, light rum and ginger beer with Hillary sitting next to him, he almost forgot why he was here.

***

John Storm fought the mosquitos, braver now that the sun had set, and worked the cramps from his thighs. He had been waiting for several hours and seen nothing unusual, but this kind of work took time. You never knew when you would catch the break you needed, and just as his patience was expiring, he heard the soft drone of a helicopter in the distance. It moved closer, and he brought the glasses to bear on the deck of the ship. Cyrus and his guests were gathered in a tight group on the top deck, their eyes to the sky.

The single-rotor chopper banked and slowed over the ship, gently lowering itself a few feet at a time until it rested on the top deck. The engines wound down, and he watched the Iranian duck and move toward the cockpit. He opened the clear glass door, and the first thing Storm saw was the stiletto heels of the occupant, followed by perfect legs and the rest of the body to match. The woman took his hand and exited the chopper. He couldn't help but notice there was not a hair out of place on her head as they moved to the waiting group where the fake, touchless hugs of the rich were exchanged. He looked back to the chopper and watched the pilot, who took several designer bags from the back and then two other cases that were clearly not designer or luggage.

He smiled, the wait having paid off, and studied the cases. They were identical in size and clearly contained something valuable. Before he could notice any further details, two uniformed crewmen took them from the pilot's hand before he could set them on the deck. With cautious looks, they carried them inside. John moved his gaze back to the group, trying to place the woman, who by her looks was not someone you would forget—and when she turned, the memories came flooding back.

CHAPTER 8

Alicia was bone-tired, but the bath she craved would have to wait. After their scheduled dives, they had the first good luck in days with favorable weather to cross the Gulfstream. Customs and Immigration continued the streak and gave them a pass, allowing only a radio check as they entered US waters. Back on the dock, they said their farewells to the divers, paying special attention to the woman, who reassured them she felt fine and was very happy with the way they had handled things. Alicia was suspicious, though. Once the woman told her story to friends and family, someone always had the idea to sue.

Their arrival had coincided with the return of the afternoon dive trip run out of Cody's shop, and Alicia smiled as the returning passengers quizzed the divers about their Bahamas adventure. Everything she overheard was positive, and she texted the clerk working inside to make sure there were plenty of brochures available.

"Go on," Cody said. "I'll get one of the guys to help me clean her up. Your work is more important."

She pecked him on the cheek, grabbed her laptop and eased her way past the divers talking on the dock. Taking the stairs to Cody's apartment on the side of the shop, she reached the landing and entered the combination into the door lock. A green light flashed, she heard the electronic bolt slide and she entered. The room was warm and humid. She passed through the kitchen, grabbing a bottle of water from the refrigerator, and went to the war room. This was Cody's game room, a high-tech modern design that you would never guess was here from the ramshackle appearance of the apartment.

Cold air greeted her as she opened the door. A separate ductless air-conditioning system serviced the space, always kept cool to satisfy the computer equipment. The windowless room was painted black with a grey ceiling. Sleek modern furniture sat on a rubber flooring made to reduce static and noise levels. Large monitors lined one of the walls, with several desks set back in a configuration that always reminded her of the bridge on the USS *Enterprise*. The captain's chair, as Cody called it, was in the middle of the room, with joysticks built into the arms, a keyboard mounted on a swinging stand off to the side, and of course, the obligatory drink holder.

She went to one of the desks, a new addition since she had moved in, and plugged several cables into the laptop. The screens came to life and she started pecking away at the keyboard. To most people, the rows of data would be meaningless, but this was her domain. Years in computer labs had taken her to robotics tournaments in high school, which had led to a scholarship to Stanford, where she had done her undergraduate work, and then on to MIT. With her pedigree, finding work had been easy, and she was courted by all the big Silicon Valley companies, but after a few years she had found the work unsatisfying. The rat race never stopped, developing products that were obsolete seconds after completion. Somewhere along the line, she had noticed an inner calling to do something good, and when the CIA had offered her employment, she'd bitten the bullet, accepting the minuscule pay rate and jumping at the opportunity.

She enjoyed the work and the challenge, but after a few years, the monotony of cubicle life made her restless. Pushing thirty years old, she realized she had no life at all and started lobbying her supervisors for field work. A high-level agent in Miami had noticed her and given her a chance. But her first assignment was no training mission; the supervisor was playing both sides of the fence. Mac Travis and his sidekick Alan Trufante had opened her eyes to the world, and together they had put things right. During the operation, she had met Cody, and for the first time she'd felt fulfilled. Over the last year, she had learned to balance her obsessive need to work with the sheer joy of diving.

She sipped water and allowed her eyes to focus on the data. There was no need to concentrate as she entered a trancelike state and allowed the rows of numbers to flow. The algorithm wasn't very complicated. Although latitude and longitude appeared daunting to neophytes, it was actually quite simple once you understood it. The column on the left showed latitude, representing north and south. The next column was longitude, showing east and west. The reference line for latitude is the equator, or "0." Moving in either direction increases the number, either north or south. Longitude is a little harder to comprehend as the "0" line was placed in Greenwich, England, by the British, the ruling sea power at the time. Known as the Greenwich meridian, the numbers increase as you move away from it, followed by either an east or west notation. Key Largo, where she sat, has a position of 25 degrees, 5 minutes and 11.5 seconds north latitude and 80 degrees, 26 minutes and 50 seconds west longitude. The only other knowledge required was that a degree is sixty nautical miles, a minute translates to roughly a mile, and a second is around one hundred feet.

The numbers running across the screen were in the British Virgin Islands. Each position had a corresponding value next to it representing a call being made to a number outside of the area—one requiring a satellite to transmit. She concentrated on the coordinates near 18 degrees 30 minutes north and 64 degrees 20 minutes west—Virgin Gorda, where the *Shahansha* was currently located. Some numbers remained stagnant, indicating calls in progress, while others appeared and disappeared as calls were made and disconnected. Before SIM cards and the ease of using cell phones for international calls, this had been easy, but now it required complex programing to sort out the calls. A map of the island was on another screen, and she punched a series of keys to superimpose the lat/lon grid over it. Soon the numbers running by started to form a pattern, and her trained mind could place any signal coming from Virgin Gorda to within a hundred feet.

It was mindless for her, and she allowed her subconscious to do the work. She knew the Iranian's yacht was anchored there, but had no idea if he was on it. He was crafty enough that the ship could be a decoy. But soon enough she would know. His need for constant communication was one of his signatures and would allow her to track his movements. A third screen came to life, showing satellite surveillance of the bay where the boat was docked. It was hard to miss the yacht, but her feed did not allow her enough data to see any detail of the decks or manipulate the satellite.

She jumped when Cody came up from behind and hugged her neck, kissing her forehead. It had been a rough charter, and she knew she should spend some quality time with him, but they both knew this was it. They either completed this contract or they were in for a major lifestyle change—maybe requiring day jobs. She touched his forearm.

"You can have the other screens." She shut off the satellite and map views. "I just need to watch the numbers."

He grunted, "No. You gotta do your thing. This is real life, I don't need to be playing games."

She turned away from the monitor and looked at him, wondering for the tenth time in the last few days if she had changed his life for the worse. He used to be like a little kid; now she could see the frown lines straining to invade his face.

"Just give me a few minutes and we'll go have a glass of wine."

"Okay. I'm going downstairs to see how business has been." He kissed her again and left the room.

She rubbed her eyes. The room was dark, with only the monochromatic screen flickering as it updated. She sat back and finished the water, watching the numbers and wondering what she could do to make this right with Cody when a new line appeared. She leaned forward, having seen these numbers before. The coordinates put the call right on the Costa Smeralda dock. Before she could pull up the map, the line vanished. Forgetting Cody, she typed furiously on the keyboard and opened another screen with her contact database. Her trained eye went right to the number she had just seen, and she cringed unconsciously. With one phone call, this had gotten bigger than a few lines of code on the Lloyd's of London computers.

***

* * *

Mako swung his feet onto the deck of the boat and smacked his head on the low ceiling of the cabin when he heard the phone ring. Most calls he could avoid, but Alicia's distinctive ringtone was not one of them. He looked over at Hillary, sleeping fully clothed on top of the sheet, and hoped the conversation would be short. With only another day with her, he wanted every second he could get to try and break down whatever barrier was holding her back. The woman had intrigued him; her mix of self-confidence and competency had his complete attention. He had even liked it when she had scolded him about the mooring lines earlier.

He closed the door to the cabin, grabbed the phone and went to the port-side forward cabin, where he shut the door before answering. The cabin was like a sauna, but the heat was a tradeoff for the privacy. Sound carried so well over the water that if the hatch was open and the conditions were right, another boat could easily hear every word of his call. He thought about starting the motor to charge the batteries and provide additional cover, but he didn't want to wake Hillary.

"Mako here," he answered.

"Really. Who else have you stashed on board that might answer?"

He wondered for a second if she had surveillance on him right now or if it was an educated guess. Deciding on the later, he ignored the comment. "I'm guessing you didn't wake me in the middle of the night to say hi."

"If you're asleep this early, you're surely not alone," she countered.

The woman knew him too well. "Where are we?" he asked.

"The yacht is still docked at the YCCS on Virgin Gorda. But there is a complication."

"Go on," he said.

"Mei Li."

The sweltering cabin imploded on him when he heard the name of the Chinese operative. "What about her?"

"She's on his yacht."

Mako thought for a moment. He had never met the woman, but that didn't mean he didn't fear her. "She must be almost sixty now," he commented.

"Gold star for math. If she's here, there is something bigger going on than the Lloyd's code. This could be our big break," Alicia said.

"Says the woman sitting in Cody's war room. I'm here on the front line. This is not going to make things any easier," he stated, but silence hung on the phone, and he knew he was about to be dragged into waters he wasn't sure he could swim.

"Let's just see where it leads. Take the boat over to Virgin Gorda in the morning and have a look."

There was no harm in having a look, especially with the cover of the rented boat. Like a good many of the cruisers here, he would be assumed a novice sailor and would be able to get close to the yacht under that guise. "What about Storm? Does he know she's here?"

"So you did pay attention in class. Another gold star. You know he won't use a cell phone, computer or credit card when he's in the field."

The long history of Storm and Mei Li had been recounted often during his training. The two had tangled for years, neither besting the other—both, at least at one time, regarded as the top of their professions before she had disappeared and he had become obsolete.

"Call you tomorrow," Mako said and disconnected the call. He left the cabin and ascended the six steps to the deck, where he let the evening breeze dry the sweat from his body before heading back to bed.

***

Alicia clicked on Mei Li's name, focusing on the screen as the woman's latest picture and biography appeared.

"Hey, I thought you were coming out for a glass of wine?" Cody said, making her jump. "Shit. She looks delightful," he said sarcastically.

"Mei Li. Chinese operative since the seventies and probably still their best. Her face is well known enough to be on the post office wall, but somehow she is still effective."

Silence ensconced them as they read her resume from the screen.

"'Been there, done that' pretty much sums her up. But look at the list of suspected activity. Haven't they been able to pin anything on her?" Cody asked.

"She's rumored to be the daughter of a vice premier. Any action against her could start an international incident."

"What's she got to do with our contract? Looks like she'd chew up old Mako and spit him out."

"She's on Cyrus's yacht. I'm thinking about contacting Langley and telling them. There could be a bigger payoff than the Lloyd's contract," Alicia said.

Cody placed a hand on her shoulder. "Guess we won't be having that glass of wine," he said.

Alicia felt guilty, but she smelled something big. "It's for us," she said and placed her hand over his.

He left the room and she changed screens, this time opening a direct link to her contact at the CIA. He would probably not answer until morning, but she would have the initial contact, and if there was a contract in the making, that would give her the inside track. Maybe after the Agency revisited Storm and Mei Li's history, they would relieve him of the Lloyd's contract as well.

On another screen, she brought up the Iranian's profile. Scanning the information of the two operatives, she wondered what Iran and China could be up to.

CHAPTER 9

Storm did a double take, rubbed his eyes and cleaned the lenses of the field glasses with the tail of his shirt. He put the rubber cups back to his eyes and stared at the woman. It was déjà vu. She looked the same as he remembered—exactly the same. And then he realized that it couldn't be her. He calmed his breath and studied the woman. Her features were slightly subtler than her mother's, the Asian diluted by something else, and the air caught in his throat. It must be her daughter. He remembered a time when Mei Li had disappeared for several years. The word on the street was that she'd had a child then, though the father remained a mystery.

When the Iranian appeared next to her, the mystery was solved, but at the same time, things became quite a bit more complicated. The girl's Chinese blood and political lineage mixed with Cyrus's money and connections were a potent blend. Now that China was allied with Iran, the woman would wield status and power. He needed a better look, and a picture if at all possible. There was always a chance, and it happened more often than any Agency would admit, that eyewitness information was wrong. He didn't think so, but would prefer an outsider to confirm her identity. He pulled a small camera from his bag, but the range was too far. Looking around before slowly coming to his feet, he brushed off his clothes and made his way back to the road. There was nothing about his dress or look that would be appropriate for even a worker at the resort, so he stayed in the shadows of the service road by the kitchens and laundry.

He made his way uncontested to the edge of the dock, but dared go no further. Even without the uniformed guard standing by the gas dock, the area was too open and well lit. A cluster of trees near the water gave him cover as he removed the glasses again and focused on the yacht. Both figures were still there, their conversation, though he couldn't hear it, clearly heated. The woman slouched, using the natural body language that all daughters at one time or another used with their fathers to get their way, and after apparently succeeding, she left and went into the cabin. The Iranian followed a minute later, taking one case in each hand. John waited a few minutes before leaving, checked the road and headed back to the Fat Virgin restaurant.

He sat at the small bar, ordered a beer and asked the bartender to call the taxi for him. With his index and middle finger, he scraped the condensation from the bottle of Red Stripe and spread the cool water across his brow, almost missing the slightly more tolerable weather in D.C. While he waited for the water taxi, he watched a group off to the side playing a ring toss game, laughing and cajoling each other even though they were being taken for beers by a younger man with a Dutch accent. He envied their freedom.

It had been a long day, and he wanted a nightcap and his bed. Finally the water taxi arrived. He paid his tab and went to the dock, where he boarded the boat and told the driver his destination.

***

* * *

Mako woke slowly, the rum from last night clearly having an effect on him. He was naked and alone. Kicking his legs, he untangled himself from the sheets crammed in the foot of the V-berth. The smell of coffee brewing in the galley motivated him enough to pull on his board shorts and move aft. He poured a cup and, balancing it in his hand, he made his way up to the cockpit, where Hillary was laid out in the sun.

"Hey, sailor. About time you got up. Your phone's been beeping like crazy and I gotta go," she said and sat up.

Mako stared at her cleavage as she moved, barely able to take his eyes away. "Let me check in and we'll get going."

"You're moving a little slow this morning. Do what you have to. I can handle the boat," she said and rose.

He sat there for a minute and drank the dark brew before going back into the cabin and grabbing his phone. Hillary was moving around him, closing hatches and setting the cabin in order before their departure. The screen was full of texts, mainly from Alicia. It sounded like she had information for him, but there was nowhere to talk in private. It would have to wait until he dropped Hillary off.

Without the breeze blowing in the hatches, the cabin quickly turned into a sauna. He took the phone and moved back to the cockpit.

"Can you give me a hand?" she asked.

The motor turned over, and she set it in neutral and revved it to two thousand RPMs to give the batteries a charge.

He set the phone down. "Sure."

"Go forward and release the mooring line. I'll get us out of here."

He stumbled forward, using the stays for support, skirting the narrow path between the cabin and rail. At the bow, he untied one end and pulled it through the eye of the mooring line. They were free of the ball now, and he heard the transmission click into reverse. Grabbing the rail to keep from falling as the boat jerked backwards, he fell to his knees. On the deck, he coiled the line and crawled back to the cabin.

She spun the boat, and he found himself looking at the large island of Tortola, dead ahead. Hillary steered a serpentine course through the mooring field, carefully avoiding the other boats. She cleared the last ball and turned toward the north.

"What's up? Road Harbor's over there, isn't it?" Mako asked, pointing to the barely distinguishable harbor to the west.

"Your little party last night has me running a bit late. I'm going to head to Marina Cay, and you can run me over to the airport in the dinghy," she said. "Think you can handle the mainsail?"

He looked back at her. "You bet," he said, dreading another trip forward. He grabbed the stay and crawled to the mast while she turned the bow into the wind.

"Okay," she yelled from the cockpit. "Just pull the halyard."

He looked at the mess of lines attached to the mast, trying to figure out what she was talking about. Actual sailing had not been in his plan when he'd chartered the boat. He had wanted the boat for cover, not sport.

She must have noticed his indecision. "The black one. Pull it hand over hand."

He found the line, unwound it from the cleat and started to pull. Slowly the sail rose. She called him back to the protection of the cockpit and turned the wheel to starboard.

"Here." She pointed to the winch handle. "Crank it up the rest of the way with this."

The sail caught the wind, and she settled on a course while Mako turned the handle, tightening the line an inch at a time.

"There you go," she said and reached over, released the furling line and pulled on the jib sheet.

With both sails out and the assistance of the engine, the boat picked up speed, slamming through the waves as they crossed the Sir Francis Drake passage. An hour later, after he had fumbled his way through several tacking maneuvers, she turned into the wind again, released the jib sheet and pulled in the jib furling line. The sail wrapped around itself, and she secured the lines.

"Why don't you hold her into the wind?" She offered him the wheel and moved forward, climbing onto the forward deck without any support. "Release the black line and feed the slack to me," she called back.

He reached over and lifted the catch on the mechanism, freeing the halyard, and looked up surprised to see her climbing the mast. She was several feet above the deck, pulling down the sail and folding it back on itself into the cover.

"Hey! The wind. Steer into the wind," she yelled.

Having no idea where the wind was from, he turned the wheel to the port side . He stared at her lithe body, relieved that he had turned the right way. She finished lashing the sail, dropped the four feet to the deck, and entered the cockpit. Flashing a brief smile, she slid past him to pull in the dinghy line. After pointing out the course into the harbor, she went below, emerging a few minutes later in her uniform.

Mako offered his phone number when she hopped onto the pier at Trellis Bay.

"Why don't we make this interesting? There's a bar called Corsair's over in Jost Van Dyke. Write something on the wall for me," she said, and blew him a kiss.

He watched her walk across the tarmac and into the terminal before reversing the engine and starting back in the direction of the boat. It wasn't often a woman made him feel this way—inferior but wanting more. Deciding he needed a diversion, he took a detour to the small island of Marina Cay. Speeding through the mooring field, he brushed off the angry looks from the other boaters. After tying the dinghy to the dock, he climbed the hill to the bar and ordered a shot with a beer chaser.

After a few Red Stripes and some casual flirting with the barmaid, he was feeling more himself and realized he had left his phone on the boat. He paid for the beers and ambled back down the hill to the dinghy dock. After a quick run through the mooring field, he tied up to the sailboat and climbed aboard.

Regretting that he had not bought any beer on the island, he opened a bottle of water, ignored the messages on the screen, and pressed the contact button for Alicia. She answered right away, and after subjecting him to a brief scolding, she calmed down enough to talk.

"Virgin Gorda. There's a yacht club at the entrance to Biras Creek." She paused. "Do you think you can find it?"

Though the barb hit home, he ignored it. "Right on. I'll be there tonight. Check in with you then."

"I emailed a packet that you might want to have a look at. Mei Li is on the yacht."

He had first heard the name and the legendary stories at the academy. He disconnected, promising her he would read the dossier after he moored—and had a beer. After releasing the line from the mooring ball, he climbed back to the cockpit, where he pushed the throttle forward and reversed course out of the harbor.

Under motor, he followed the GPS plotter, staying clear of the Dog Islands, and then turned north in the direction of Virgin Sound. Further out to sea, he saw the sails of a handful of boats tacking back and forth toward the same destination, but fortunately there were a half dozen other motor sailors plowing directly to the inlet, and he fell in line, content to let them do the navigation for him.

The convoy entered the bay around two, and he checked the chart plotter, finding Biras Creek dead ahead. He cruised past several smaller bays and saw the long, pristine dock of the YCCS, bigger and more brash than Alicia had described it. Several large yachts were tied to her black pilings. There were more slips empty than full, and he wondered if he would be in a better position if he docked there rather than tying up to a mooring buoy in the narrow inlet beyond the yacht club. Shore power decided it for him, and he set the throttle to neutral and went for the VHF. The dockmaster gave him the exorbitant rate, which he flinched at but agreed to, hoping Alicia was not mad enough to cut off his credit card.

Several uniformed men waited for him at the assigned slip, which he couldn't help but notice was well away from the larger yachts. He waved off their help. Pulling bow first into the slip, he crashed into a piling before one of the men jumped aboard and took control of the boat. The other men quickly tied off the lines and hooked up the fresh water and shore power. Mako thanked them, shut off the engine and went below, where he showered and changed. With his phone in hand, he texted Alicia that he had arrived, neglecting to tell her that he had changed the plan or mention the cost of the slip.

He strode casually up the dock to the paved walkway that led up a slight incline to a large building. A large Rolex clock hung over the entrance, making him feel slightly self-conscious that his shirt was not tucked in. But he knew the Vineyard Vines attire he sported would be welcomed here. He reached for the large glass door, pulled it open, and entered the luxurious lobby. With a nod, he passed the woman at the check-in counter and walked into the bar. Several groups were scattered around the room overlooking the North Sound. Not one head turned when he entered and sat at the bar. A uniformed bartender with a permanent smile came toward him, giving him a look like he didn't belong.

"Are you staying with us, sir?" he asked.

"I am," Mako responded and pointed vaguely to his rented boat.

"All right, then. What can I get for you?"

"Pusser's and soda with a lime," Mako ordered.

His look still unsure, the bartender nodded and made the drink. Mako thanked him, took a sip and hit the email button on his phone. He glanced down at the message from Alicia and took a deep drink while the attachment loaded. The Wi-Fi was surprisingly slow for such a resort, but the file finally loaded. He finished the drink, signaled the bartender and waited for a refill before looking at it.

CHAPTER 10

The bartender moved down the bar. "Get you another?"

Mako shook his head. "Not my kinda place, if you know what I mean. Anywhere else around that gets a little more action?"

"There's the Bitter End." He pointed across the water. "Or Leverick's. I'm thinking that'd be more to your liking. Lots of young ladies there off the boats."

Mako did a double take when the bill was placed in front of him. He did his best to disguise his shock and removed his credit card, wondering how he was going to justify this to Alicia. He looked through the open doors at Virgin Sound. From his vantage point, he could see the pyramid roofs of the Bitter End to his right and Saba Rock, a small island with a marina, restaurant, and bar, across the way. Leverick's was around several points and not visible from here.

"Can I take the dinghy over?"

The bartender looked at the water. "Not too choppy, probably be alright tonight. Just take a light with you."

Mako thanked him and left the bar. He passed back through the lobby, catching a few looks, and walked to the sailboat. Once aboard, he thought about moving the boat to the moorings or docks at Leverick's, but decided against doing in the fading light what he could barely do during the day.

He climbed into the dinghy and started the engine. After releasing the painter, he pulled the lever to forward, turned the throttle on the steering arm and sped away from the dock. The water was calm, making for an easy run across the bay. It took only a few minutes to cover the mile between resorts, and he smiled as he turned past Clark Rock and saw the lights of the marina and hotel in front of him. Reggae music came from the bar, and even from here he could see the crowd of suntanned tourists. This was more his kind of place, he thought. The dinghy dock was crowded. Another sign the bartender had steered him right. He copied the other boaters, dropping the small anchor off the stern after pushing two of the small grey inflatables aside to make enough room for him to tie up.

Graceful was not how you would describe his transition from the dinghy to the dock. Forced to take a knee in order to gain his footing, he rose, brushed off his crawfish-patterned shorts, and headed past the pool to the bar. White smiles contrasted with the tanned faces lining the busy bar. The high-top tables were full, and several couples were dancing barefoot in the sand. He found a gap at the bar, turned and slid sideways into the space, where he watched the crowd while waiting for one of the bartenders to see him. An older lady slid over a seat, giving him his own space and a wink that offered more, but thankfully the bartender interrupted.

After ordering a Pusser's and soda, he pulled out his phone to check Alicia's email. After all, if she was paying for his drinks, he was still working.

He glanced down at the file and scrolled through several pages of text before he came to the first picture, but before he could look back, a woman entered the bar who drew the attention of everyone sitting there. It took all his willpower not to stare at the stunning Eurasian woman casually walking past him. She glanced in his direction, but he averted his eyes and looked at the picture on his phone.

The bartender was already there when the woman pulled out a chair three places down from him and sat. "Can I get you one of our famous Painkillers, miss?" he asked, emphasizing his island accent.

"No, thank you," she said. "A double shot of your best tequila with a lime."

He turned away and perused the bottles on the top shelf. Mako looked up from his phone and glanced at her, then looked back down and did a double take. It was the same woman as in the picture—just thirty years younger.

With one eye on the woman and another on the phone, he scanned the biography of the elder agent, Mei Li. It was a thorough background, but there were chunks of time missing—mostly her childbearing years. He read further, but there was no mention of children. Another glance at the woman and he knew, whether she was in the file or not, this was her daughter. Now, the question was what to do with the information. He drank and watched her down the tequila and place the glass down on the bar. A moment of panic overtook him, not knowing what to do if she left. Did he follow her or let her go? Was it worth the risk to be seen?

The questions answered themselves when she got up and moved to the dance floor. Stepping down to the sandy surface, she kicked off her flip-flops and started dancing barefoot in the sand. This was his style of surveillance, and he decided to chance an encounter. He set his drink down and walked over to the sandy area. Kicking off his boat shoes, he moved next to her and started to sway with the music. Not copying her, but letting her know he was there. She smiled and turned her body toward him, a signal he read to move closer. Together they synced their bodies, moving to the mellow music of Harry Belafonte singing "Jamaica Farewell."

The song ended, and they stood looking at each other. "Buy you a drink?" Mako said, reverting to the time-honored line.

"That'd be nice," she said. "A double tequila, and bring it back here. I want to dance."

He backed away from her, watching her move. Her arms swung over her head, accentuating her hips as they moved back and forth. So entranced was he that he crashed into the older woman who had offered her seat. Returning to the sand, he handed her the drink. She wrapped her arms around him, and he turned to face her.

***

Storm walked into the bar and stared in shock. It was louder and more crowded than his liking, but he saw a woman dancing by herself and instantly recognized her from the yacht. Reversing course, he walked to the crowded bar, watching the woman, when a man walked up to her and handed her a drink. A frown crossed his face.

He watched as they touched glasses and brushed their faces together, stopping just short of a kiss. Laughing, they sipped their drinks and started dancing. He frowned, wondering what to do about this development. Play it out and use Mako to see what the woman and the Iranian were up to, or warn him of the danger he was in. He knew Mako's modus operandi, but also knew of his naivety—especially around beautiful women. He couldn't help but notice the couple had that magical look about them, and he decided he needed to break this up before it went too far. He sat and drank, waiting for the right time, but the longer he sat, the more frustrated he became watching Mako operate. If he was only as dedicated to his profession as he was to womanizing, he could be a top-notch agent. As it was, he somehow fumbled through enough successes to get by, but Storm knew he had the best backup in the world. Alicia Phon had been known in the intelligence community as the go-to analyst. But he knew all too well what budget cuts and appeasing politicians had done to the Agency. Like himself and so many others, she was "self-employed" now. Word was that since she had left the Agency, she was shacked up with some dive guy in Key Largo and did contract work as it suited her.

From the way their bodies were intertwined, Mako and the woman looked like they would soon need some privacy. He needed to do something now. Storm finished his drink, paid and left a generous tip. Generous enough to beg forgiveness for what he was about to do. He left the bar, moved into the shadows of the walkway near the pool and waited. It was not long before he saw them coming towards him. Mako was on the pool side, making his plan easier to execute.

***

The woman had sucked his attention, focusing it like a straw as she drank his soul. Forgetting why he was here, or rather rationalizing that this was intelligence gathering, he went willingly. Never asking the question that should have been crossing his mind: *Should I be getting involved with the daughter of Mei Li?* He'd felt chemistry before, but this was like a nuclear reaction, and he found himself totally under her spell.

The song ended and she tugged his hand, leading him off the

sand, and after quickly finding their shoes, she whispered in his ear a promise of something he couldn't refuse. They left the bar hand in hand and were about to pass the pool when a figure shot out of the shadows. For a brief second, the light caught his face and Mako froze.

Before he could react, he lost his balance and felt the woman's hand slip from his grip. A split second later, he was in the pool, clawing to the surface. He spat the water from his mouth and stared at the gathering crowd. A bouncer pushed the onlookers aside and helped him out of the water. He shook himself off and scanned the faces watching him, but the woman was gone. The bouncer was encouraging the crowd to break up, but out of the corner of his eye, he saw John Storm moving up the stairs to the hotel.

His night over, he slunk toward the dinghy dock, where he untied the dock line and started the engine. Seconds before the stern anchor line got sucked into the propeller, he retrieved it before embarrassing himself again. Just as he turned into the main bay, the dinghy was assaulted by the wake of a water taxi speeding by, and he remembered the bartender's advice to use a light. He was close enough to see the woman in the light of the cockpit looking ahead, oblivious to the dinghy riding the wake in the dark. It was too late to avoid the waves, and he eased off the throttle and coasted, watching the taxi move away.

While he rode out the swells from the water taxi, he remembered the woman with the wonderful accent who had done the boat orientation in Tortola mentioning something about a plastic case. Moving to the bow, he opened the small storage compartment, which yielded a watertight container. He emptied the contents onto the deck and found a small LED light. The wake was past now, and with the light held high in one hand, he opened the throttle and sped across the flat water to the sailboat. Back in the cabin, he changed clothes, realizing when he pulled his phone from the pocket of the wet shorts that it was ruined. The only means of communication available was the VHF radio, which might be great for a weather check or in an emergency, but to contact Alicia, he needed something more secure.

He went on deck and studied the surrounding area. The lights of Bitter End twinkled just across the water, and he remembered reading something in the cruising guide about them having amenities for cruisers. He hopped into the dinghy, hoping that a private payphone would be one of them.

***

John sat on the bed in his room, staring down at his phone and wondering whether to make the call. He was pretty sure that Mako had not seen him, but although the younger agent's tradecraft left a lot to be desired, he couldn't be sure. He would move forward under the assumption that he had been seen by both Mako and the woman. Chance was not something that he wanted to rely on.

Deciding that action was the best recourse, he put the phone aside. If his cover was blown, he needed to know. Being identified by Mako would inconvenience the operation. He changed his clothes, grabbed the field glasses and left the room, walking toward the hotel exit higher up the road. Across the street was a small store, where he grabbed a few energy bars, a bottle of water and mosquito repellent.

Deciding that a water taxi was too conspicuous, he opted to liberate a dinghy. Staying in the shadows, he crossed to the pier and made his way to the dock. There were at least a dozen identical craft tied up, distinguished only by their numbers. He knew it was commonplace for people to take the wrong dinghy, and the rental companies would provide a ready replacement knowing the missing boat would be found sooner or later.

He stepped down into the last craft in the line and went to the small outboard. Engines this size did not have keys. All that was needed was a spacer to deactivate the dead-man switch. Digging in his pocket, he took a bill and folded it into a horseshoe shape, using it to open the gap required for the engine to start. In case of a real man overboard, the driver would, in theory, have a lanyard looped around his or her wrist which would pull the spacer, cutting the engine if they went overboard.

The engine started, and he released the line, glancing back at the pier to see if the theft had been noticed. No one was looking his way, so he pushed the lever back to reverse and eased the dinghy back. Once he cleared the other boats, he clicked the lever to forward, accelerated and headed toward the mooring field. He navigated a circuitous route through the moored boats to confuse any onlooker before turning into the sound and speeding towards the yacht club.

CHAPTER 11

“What do you mean, he pushed you into the pool and now your phone’s wrecked?”

Mako held the receiver away from his ear while Alicia’s rant continued.

“And calling collect? Nobody calls collect anymore. I didn’t even know they still offered it. And you found a pay phone. Nice, like this call is not going to be on the NSA hot sheet.”

He knew she was almost out of steam and bit his tongue. “What about the woman?” Imagining her fingernails tapping on a keyboard, he waited, watching the cruisers come and go from the shower stalls next to the phone.

“Doesn’t exist. There’s a gap in Mei Li’s history that would account for a child. But no details,” Alicia said.

“I’m telling you, she’s a cross between that Cyrus dude and the picture you sent me. A dead match.”

“And how close did you get to determine that?” she asked.

Mako paused again, wondering if she had cameras on him or if it was another educated guess. “Funny. Wouldn’t mind getting to know her, though.”

The line was silent for a moment. “You know, of all your half-baked ideas, that’s not a bad one. Stay away from the yacht, though. Cyrus would recognize you after London."

"You might want to send that memo to John Storm. He's here," Mako said.

"How does he do it?" Alicia asked.

"Hell if I know, but he's the one that pushed me into the pool."

"Like that's the whole story." She paused. "Let me get to work on this."

"What about a phone?"

The line went dead, and he replaced the receiver. He didn't need to ask permission. The water might have ruined the phone, but it hadn't bothered his credit card. Tomorrow he'd head over to Spanish Town and get a replacement. Tonight, however, he needed to do some work.

He left the dock area and went back to the dinghy. Across the water, he could see the yacht, its lights casting a reflection on the water, and decided to take a run over for a closer look. The inflatable skimmed across the flat water, and he extinguished the light just before reaching the yacht club. He coasted up to an empty section of the marina and dropped into neutral while he evaluated the dock area. The yacht glowed in the darkness, and he could hear people talking, but he was too low in the water to see anything. He reversed course, trying to back up enough to get a better view, when he saw what looked like a garage door open at the boat's stern and a speedboat slide backwards into the water. The yacht's dinghy might have been the dream boat for many, but looking at it with the backdrop of the yacht, the twin-engine twenty-plus-foot boat seemed so small.

The voices moved to the rear deck, and he could see two women standing by the transom. One was the woman from the bar; the other looked like she could be her sister, but Mako knew it was her mother—Mei Li. A uniformed man skillfully pulled the boat alongside the yacht and waited there while the women boarded. Mako realized he was exposed now that they were on the same level. He ducked and pulled the dinghy under the closest dock and out of sight, waiting there until the man pushed the speedboat away from the yacht and accelerated into the night.

The night was dark, and Mako could easily see the white anchor light of the boat as it sped away. Pulling the dinghy from its hiding place, he sped after them, knowing he had no chance to catch them. He just wanted to keep them in sight. The speedboat passed the Bitter End and headed toward several dots of light marking the resort and marina at Saba Rock. He arrived at the dock just in time to see the women step out of the speedboat and enter the restaurant.

"What the hell are you doing?" a voice came out of the darkness.

He turned to see John Storm in a dinghy almost identical to his.

"Following them. The same as you, I suspect. And thanks, by the way, for ruining my shot at her."

"You fool. You have no idea what you're dealing with. There's venom running through her mother's veins, and I suspect it's the same for the daughter," Storm said.

Mako stared at him. "And why the concern?"

"You blow your cover, they'll be on alert and make things difficult for me."

"So, I'm just supposed to go away and leave you to collect on the contract?" Mako wondered why the older agent had even shown himself.

"In a perfect world, yes. But there's more going on here than you or your techie partner know. This could be big enough for both of us."

Mako was not sure what to say. It was out of character for Storm to work with anyone else—especially him. He tried to decide if this was a deception or if he was sincere—or how badly he needed Alicia. "Go on," he said.

"Go on what? Are you in or out?"

He had nothing to lose. "In. What'd you have?"

"Let's get out of here before they see us. Meet me at the dinghy dock at the Bitter End," Storm said and started his outboard.

Mako watched him speed away, wondering if he should follow. There really was nothing to lose. With the women in the restaurant on Saba Rock, he expected the yacht would remain here overnight. He started the engine and followed Storm into the night.

They tied up next to each other at the Bitter End.

"You be needin' the phone again?" the dockmaster asked Mako.

He shook his head and followed Storm to the bar. They sat at a corner table with their backs to the wall in typical spy fashion and ordered beers and chips. Storm drained half his glass before talking. In a hushed voice, he told Mako about Mei Li and the two cases he had seen offloaded from the helicopter.

"We know about the mom-and-daughter team," Mako said.

"How does that digital ninja of a partner of yours know this stuff?" Storm asked. "I saw it with my own eyes. She's a thousand miles away and figures it out."

Mako didn't bother to answer. In truth, he had no idea how she did it either. "So, about the cases. Are you thinking this is above and beyond the contract?"

Storm finished his beer and waved for the check. "Only one way to find out, and that's to see what they have." He got up, fished a bill out of his pocket and dropped it on the table. "Coming?"

Mako was surprised by the invitation from a man who typically scorned him. He got up and followed Storm from the bar to the dinghy dock.

"We'll take yours. They might be out looking for mine by now," he said and stepped down to the dinghy.

With the weight of both men, the soft-sided boat was heavier in the water, causing Mako to adjust the throttle to stop the spray coming over the bow as it slammed into the small waves. Mako steered to a spot that Storm pointed out near another yacht that would give them cover.

"Are we going aboard?" Mako asked, as the inflatable gunwale hit the dock a little harder than he would have liked.

"Not we. I'll go. You stay here," Storm said and jumped onto the dock.

Before Mako could reply, Storm had disappeared into the shadows. He sat on the pier with his feet on the dinghy, thinking about what he had landed in now. Working with Storm was a little like playing Russian roulette with every chamber loaded. He'd had a reputation in the old days as a star, but had been released from the Agency for his cowboy antics. They got the job done, but the trail of collateral damage he left behind him was unacceptable to the suits in D.C.

Mako looked over at the yacht, sitting quietly at the pier, when suddenly an alarm went off and the yacht lit up. Floodlights hit the deck and surrounding water, and he saw a splash off the bow. He jumped down into the dinghy and fired the engine, taking off in the direction of the disturbance. Steering close to the yacht's hull, which blocked much of the light, he was able to stay out of sight until he saw Storm swimming away. Gunshots came from the bow. He was out of range of the lights now, but not the bullets. Mako looked back at the gunmen and opened up the throttle, steering for the swimmer. Storm was ten feet ahead of the dinghy when the bullet hit.

Air hissed from the inflatable sides of the dinghy just as Storm grabbed the line running around the gunwales.

"Gun it!" he yelled.

Bullets struck around the boat, at least one hitting the other side. With its sides deflating rapidly, even with the throttle opened all the way, the boat dragged through the water, and with Storm being pulled behind, they were slowly sinking. Going back to the sailboat was out of the question. The men on the yacht would see them for sure. Instead he chose the closest dock and the protection of Biras Creek.

By the time they covered the quarter mile to the dock of the Fat Virgin, the dinghy's sides had collapsed, leaving only the deck to keep them afloat. Without bothering to tie up, Mako jumped onto the dock and extended an arm down to Storm, who ignored it and climbed onto the dock.

"What kind of cowboy shit was that?" Storm said, spitting seawater at Mako.

"That was saving-your-ass cowboy shit," Mako spat back.

"I was fine. You blew our cover completely. Now they know where to look for us."

Mako looked down again, knowing he would be unable to please the man. "What now?"

"There."

A water taxi had just pulled up to the dock and several partiers boarded. Before the driver could close the chain across the entrance, Mako and Storm boarded after them.

"Got a call from Saba Rock. Only stop is the rock," the man said in a singsong accent.

Mako was about to speak when Storm looked at him and then moved his eyes to the other passengers, indicating they should wait until they were out of earshot. They rode in silence, dodging the curious looks from the two other couples. Finally the taxi dropped them at the pier. Before they had a chance to talk, they saw the two women leave the building and head toward the dock. Both men ducked behind the gunwale when they approached.

"Where to now? Great idea to come here," Mako whispered, risking a look at the speedboat waiting to take the women back to the yacht. The driver was on his phone, talking to someone who sounded like he was ordering him to get the women and find the man who had escaped the ship. Once they boarded, he set the phone down, cast off the lines and gunned the engines.

Storm reached in his pocket and pulled out a wad of wet money. He peeled off a twenty-dollar bill and handed it to the driver. "Can you get us back to the Virgin and stay out of sight of the speedboat?"

"They be looking for you? Running away from women gets expensive," he laughed and reversed the boat, spinning the wheel when it cleared the dock. "Clock's running—where to?"

"Bitter End," Storm said and turned to Mako. "We can grab the dinghy we left there and sneak over to the boat."

The driver stayed between the mooring field and the shore leading to the Bitter End. Mako looked ahead at the speedboat circling the harbor, thinking they would be screened by the moored boats, but suddenly it picked up speed and started toward them.

"They're coming toward us. How did they know?"

"Didn't you see the dockmaster giving us the eye at Saba Rock? He must have radioed them. I'm sure there's a bounty on us."

"What do you boys want me to do?" the driver asked.

"We have to lose them," Mako said.

"You got the cash, I can accommodate you."

Mako nodded, hoping he took credit cards, and was pulled backwards as the driver gunned the engine and spun the wheel. The speedboat reacted to them and followed.

"How's this going to work? They're gaining on us," Mako yelled over the engine noise.

"Not to worry, boys, though you'll have a bit of a hike."

The three men crowded around the helm as the driver headed toward a small gap to the side of the island. Mako turned around and saw the speedboat holding its distance, probably wondering what they were up to. This water was shoal-ridden and dangerous. Unless you were familiar with it, there was a high probability of grounding or sinking. The driver had a smile on his face as he sped through a narrow channel to the left of the Saba Rock. Even in the dark, they could see the silt kicked up by the propeller, and they watched the speedboat hesitate. Mako thought he heard a woman yell an order, and the boat took off after them.

The three men turned around and watched the speedboat dig in when the driver gunned the motors. If they had maintained speed, they could have made it through the shallows with the boat on plane, but their hesitation had cost them, and the bow lifted high, digging the engines into the muck.

"Looks like you boys got some luck, then," the driver chuckled. "They'll be there for a bit." He spun the wheel and steered a wide circle around the shallows, reentering the bay through deeper water. Mako looked over at the speedboat; even from this distance, he saw the glares of the women staring at them. Fortunately, Storm had turned off the cabin light, leaving them in darkness, invisible to the other boat.

CHAPTER 12

Mako woke sometime after dawn. It was overcast, but from the glow of the sun still penetrating the clouds, he knew it was well into the morning. He reached for his phone, cursing Storm when he remembered it had been ruined. Agency protocol was for anyone in the field to always wear a watch, but they irritated his wrist, and he wasn't sure how the old rules applied to him now. Getting a new phone was the one and only thing on his list today. Storm had told him he would keep an eye on the yacht, though he got the feeling it wasn't an agreed-on decision. The older agent clearly distrusted his abilities—as if he could care. Results mattered, and although his methods might look bumbling and lucky to other agents, he got results, even if he was in denial about how much Alicia had to do with his success. Her reputation was such that they said she could direct a monkey through a pharaoh's tomb and bring him back alive.

Deciding on a more sublime dress than the Vineyard Vines outfit, he chose khaki shorts and a Hawaiian button-down shirt. He asked the dockmaster to call a cab for him and told him he would be back later to vacate the slip. Even he had trouble swallowing the dock fees. The open-air cab showed up a few minutes later, and the driver motioned him to the bench seats in back. The pink cab sat in the shade of the porte cochere, waiting for an elderly couple who climbed in and sat across from him. The driver opened the sliding rear window of the cab and asked them if they were buckled up; then, without waiting for a response, he slammed the transmission into forward and sped up the hill. Once they were out of the gates, the road degraded quickly, and the three passengers realized the importance of the safety check.

The cab hugged the steel barriers guarding the hillsides as it climbed to the top of the island. Mako was white-knuckled holding the seat and did a double take, cringing every time a car passed. Despite his time in England, this wrong-side-of-the-road stuff on narrow winding hills was disconcerting. He was momentarily distracted from the ride when the cab crested the hill, allowing the occupants a three-hundred-sixty-degree view of the island. The driver stopped and opened the window, giving a brief tour of their surroundings from the comfort of the air-conditioned cab. Behind them lay the North Sound, where they had come from. Mosquito Island guarded the entrance. Richard Branson of Virgin fame was building an ecolodge there, he explained. To their right was Sir Francis Drake Bay, with a chain of smaller islands falling off to the south.. Tortola lay across the other side. Sails dotted the water's surface. On the left lay the Caribbean Sea, white-capped and angry looking even from here.

The thirty-second tour over, he closed the window and sped down the hill. If they thought the ride up was harrowing, the ride down was worse. The couple exchanged looks of distress bonding them together as they made their descent to Spanish Town. Finally the road leveled and houses started to appear. They were close together, many built in the third-world fashion: single-story concrete buildings with rebar sticking out of the roofs, waiting for the next generation to grow up and have kids before adding a second story. They reached the main street and Mako hopped out. The cab pulled away, with the older couple talking excitedly about the Baths, a national park further south. Something about huge boulders that held not the least bit of interest to him.

Half an hour later, he was walking toward the marina with a new phone in his hand. The waitress at a small cafe let him charge the battery while he ate breakfast. Finished, he moved outside and waited while it powered up, then pressed the icon for the web browser. His contact list was lost, and he knew Alicia would scold him for never backing anything up. Without the numbers, he searched the Internet for Cody's dive shop's page. It came up, and he hit the call button. After pleading with the man who answered that he really was a personal friend, he was told that Cody was out on a charter, but Alicia was upstairs. The man took his number and said he would let her know.

While he waited for a call back, he walked down to the dock looking for the harbormaster, much preferring a water-based ride back to his boat.

***

Alicia looked down at the piece of paper with a hastily written phone number she didn't recognize. After a long morning of texting, calling and emailing him, it appeared Mako had bought a new phone and not had the sense to port his old number or call her to help. She took a deep breath and dialed.

"Ah, when was the last time I told you how wonderful you are?" he answered, hoping to defuse her anger. "And so sweet—"

She knew that he was not referring to her voice, often called shrill, a bad Asian mix, she guessed. "I suppose you have a story," she cut him off.

He started rambling about the same thing as last night, but her attention picked up when he told the story of the chase.

"Not to worry, we're partners now."

Those words were enough to put her over the edge. Partnering with John Storm was a suicide mission. "And you made this decision unilaterally?"

"Uni-what? I had to do something. My phone got wrecked in the pool."

She tried to control her temper, thinking it would be easier to get a primate to do his job. "Now slow down and give me everything." She hit several keys, and a red light appeared on the screen to record the conversation. "Start to finish."

Mako told his story. It sounded more like a soap opera than a mission. When he finished, she asked him to share his location in the phone's settings and waited while the map loaded, showing a small blue dot in Spanish Town.

"So, mamasan, what's our next move?" he asked.

She sat back and thought before answering. "Go back and get that damned boat out of the yacht club. Put it on a mooring ball near the Bitter End and text me." That ought to give her several hours to come up with a plan. In fact, she had been working most of the night, between his seeming disappearance and a strange signal coming from the yacht. His mention of Storm seeing two cases being brought aboard had started to fill in the blanks.

Although not under contract to find out what was in the cases, she was monitoring all communications from the yacht, piecing together the crew and guests from their emails, texts, and Facebook posts. The yacht club, for all its exclusivity, had a primitive Wi-Fi network. She turned toward the captain's chair. Cody had just run a program he had developed, an algorithm stronger than any she had seen to break the passwords of the gamers he played against. It had astonished her the level of obsessive competition of his peers, taking the game to levels never thought of by the developers. The goal of the program was to hack into another player's system and leave a piece of code that would spy on and report their moves.

Cody quickly found the password. "YCCS—Yacht Club Costa Smeralda."

She laughed at the simplicity of the rich.

It only took her a few minutes from there to assemble a profile of the people onboard. There were six crew, all easily identifiable from their Facebook posts. The Iranian never left a digital footprint, but Mako had confirmed seeing him as well as the two women. Mei Li, she had located there last night, but the daughter was a mystery. She had dug through every database she could find —nothing. It didn't matter, though; for the purposes of the mission, she would be deemed as dangerous as her mother.

The question now was, what was the mission? The original encryption data from Lloyd's, or their cargo? She suspected the cases were extremely valuable, Mei Li's presence probably tying them to China. Then there was Storm and Mako. *What an odd couple*, she thought. There was something between them that was more than the loathing they both showed for each other—some kind of rivalry. Storm, although a dinosaur, was an accomplished agent and could prove to be an asset if the conditions were right. Leaving the screen with Mako's location open, she logged into the Agency email server and started writing a proposal for the director.

***

* * *

From the same spot as yesterday, Storm had been watching the yacht since just past dawn. He brought the field glasses to his face and carefully surveyed the quiet ship. Two crewmen were busy cleaning the top deck, hosing and wiping the brilliant white fiberglass and polishing the stainless steel, but that was the only sign of life he had seen. He knew from his past surveillance that these were not morning people and relaxed, knowing they were probably still asleep. He was about to nod off himself when the roar of the engines startled him. There was a flurry of activity on the deck now, and he thought he saw the Iranian on the bridge talking to a man he suspected was the captain.

Two crewmen retrieved the dock lines, and the yacht slowly pulled forward out of the slip. Using its bow thrusters, the captain turned the ship into the open water of the sound. Storm sprung from his cover, not concerned about being seen, and ran down the dock to Mako's rented boat. It was close to noon now; he should be awake.

"Welcome aboard," Mako said from the cockpit.

"What are you doing?" He watched him playing with the phone, the box, and instructions on the bench seat beside him. For a long minute, he just stared at him before taking matters into his own hands. "Never mind. We gotta go." He went forward and untied the two bowlines, tossing them in the water instead of taking the time to slip them over the bollards, and went back to start the engine. "Get the stern lines," he ordered Mako and turned his back to the wheel.

Storm pulled out stern first before Mako had the lines off, knowing he had a few seconds to spare before he passed the pilings. Four men came running down the dock to help, but Mako was able to release the last line just before it came taut, and Storm pulled the throttle back to its limit. The exhaust gurgled behind them as he backed into his own wake, but before it could flood seawater back through the exhaust, the bow slid free of the piles. He turned around and slammed the throttle forward.

The yacht was in the distance, threading its way between the green and red pilings marking the entrance to the sound. They were falling behind, the sailboat unable to get above six knots with its small engine.

"Can you get the sails up?" he asked. Mako's look didn't inspire confidence. "Never mind. Can you follow the channel out? Green is on the right." He left the wheel to Mako and released the jib furling line. With the port sheet around the capstan, he pulled the jib out. He cranked on the winch, having to utilize its mechanical advantage to trim the sail. The boat jerked forward when the sail caught wind, the increase in speed immediate. It was not enough, though, and he grabbed the starboard stay and swung his body to the mast.

"Hold the course," he called back to Mako with a look over his shoulder to see if he was still in the channel. Waiting until they were past the point at Prickly Pear Island, he called out, "Steady now, and stay to port." His life was in Mako's hands, and he glanced back at the cockpit to make sure he was paying attention. If he swung over to starboard and passed the bow of the boat through the wind, the jib would swing over, taking him over the side. He took one more look and hauled the halyard hand over hand until the sail was three-quarters of the way up. In order to control the boom, he had left the main sheet taut, and the boat heeled over sharply as the sail caught the wind. Somehow, Mako made the adjustment and turned to starboard just enough to allow him to crawl on his hands and knees under the boom and into the cockpit.

"Nice job," he said and adjusted the sails. The yacht was out of the pass and steering a course that would take them to the east and seaward of Mosquito Island.

"You know that's Richard Branson's place. Ecolodge or something," Mako said as they followed the yacht past the island.

Storm took the wheel and shook his head.

CHAPTER 13

Alicia did her homework. Since her earliest memories, she had always known that success came from doing the work. Drilled into her by her mother, probably before preschool, she had always done whatever was needed to reach the top of her field. While she waited for a response from the CIA, she studied a white paper on the Iranian nuclear program and then pulled up a treaty just signed to defuse it. In her opinion, there were glaring holes in the process. In order to comply, Iran had to stop enriching uranium and either dilute or remove its existing supply. There were no provisions for disabling delivery mechanisms. If they were to receive enriched uranium from another country such as China, it would not be subject to inspections and could be delivered directly to the military for weaponization. She now had an idea what the cases contained, but needed to verify it. Frustrated, she got up and left the dark room, wondering why this was so apparent to her and not the politicians who had negotiated and signed the treaty. Sunlight greeted her, shocking her into reality and reminding her that she had not slept, eaten, or even used the bathroom for hours.

The clock on the microwave told her it was late morning, and she looked at the dock through the hurricane shutters, partially closed to obscure the sunlight. Both boats were out on charters, a good sign for their bottom line, but she needed Cody's help to decipher the mystery. He looked at things from an entirely different angle than she did. The difference between a gamer and an analyst. More often than she liked to admit, he had taken one look at a problem that had vexed her for hours and given her the answer. She filled a glass with water, drank it, and refilled it. The refrigerator yielded nothing of interest, and she lay down on the couch.

Sleep eluded her, and she returned to the war room. Pulling up Mei Li's biography, she opened another screen and started a timeline on a spreadsheet, placing her known activities against their locations. She found her answer soon enough and closed the bio screen. Arabic was not one of her languages, so it took some time to go back and forth with a former analyst, but they soon found the records of her daughter—Mei Lan.

***

They saw the yacht turn, now just a glimmer of white fiberglass and polished stainless steel on the blue water ahead. There had been a few tense moments when they'd thought it was going to sea, but now her destination looked like either Jost Van Dyke or St. Thomas. Mako suspected the former. There was no reason he could think of for them to enter the United States. They looked at each other, a strange feeling of camaraderie coming over them, both relieved. With no food and daylight running out, they needed to find an anchorage.

"Nice job on the provisions," Storm said. He adjusted the sails to the course change, and the boat settled on an easy beam reach.

"I was busy," Mako replied, setting down the plastic glass. He stared ahead at the yacht, now set against the outline of the island. It was miles ahead, and he lay down on the starboard bench, letting the sail shield him from the late-afternoon sun. The yacht had stayed outside of the Dog Islands and turned to the west. The hills of Jost Van Dyke were directly ahead, indistinct in the afternoon haze. Mako was sprawled on the cockpit bench and was just about asleep when the vibration from the phone startled him.

He reached into his pocket and looked at the screen. After reading the long message from Alicia, containing more detail than he cared to know, he sat up and looked at Storm.

"What's the matter? Your date for tonight canceled?" The older man laughed out loud.

Mako ignored the barb.

"Maybe you'd better let me see that," Storm said, extending his hand for the phone.

Mako complied, finding it easier to let him read it. Storm set the autopilot and read the message.

"So she found her. Mei Lan, offspring of the infamous Mei Li and Cyrus. Makes sense now why they were there. But why Jost Van Dyke?" he asked.

The chart was folded on the bench across from him, and Mako reached out and opened it. Storm stood beside him.

"Jost Van Dyke." He pointed to the large island set by itself. "Nothing there but some burnt-out hippies and a bunch of bars," Storm said.

Mako studied the chart. "There's a customs dock there," he said.

"The YCCS could have gotten them cleared from Virgin Gorda—for a few greenbacks. There has to be something else."

"Could be a decoy. Stopping only in one place here is very unusual. Maybe they're just covering their tracks—making it look like a vacation."

Storm shot him a look that could have said he was either brilliant or an idiot. He decided on the former. There was a bright side to Jost Van Dyke, he thought, remembering Hillary's challenge to leave a message on one of the bar's walls.

"As much as this pains me to say, you might be right," Storm said and went back to the wheel.

Mako lay back down and thought about his present circumstance. Being this close to Storm was a constant irritant. Not only did he feel like he was being judged every second they were together, he usually felt like he didn't measure up to whatever scale the older man used to measure him against. Unable to sleep, he pulled the phone back and texted Alicia, asking her about the state of the contract and how to proceed.

It was a good half hour before she answered, and the sun now had full dominion over the deck. He put on his sunglasses and watched Great Camanoe slide by the port side. Looking ahead, he squinted into the setting sun. The outline of Jost Van Dyke was still visible, but their prey was lost in the glare of the sun on the water.

"You have any ideas now?" Mako asked.

"Why don't you ask your girlfriend where they are? Surely she has the power to summon a satellite and get some real-time info."

Mako pecked the request into his phone. What he got back surprised him. No, she couldn't summon a satellite. The Agency had denied her request for funds, ignoring her theory. If they wanted to salvage anything out of this, they would have to get the encryption data from Cyrus.

"No go on all accounts," Mako explained the message to Storm.

"Not surprising. Those pinheads at the Agency can't see past their glasses."

"Well?" Mako asked.

"Well, what? We're stuck together—at least for now," Storm said.

Shit, Mako thought. He had to figure a way to get rid of the older agent and find the encryption data. If he could only get the girl alone….

"Pull out the cruising guide so we can pick an anchorage. These bays are dicey."

A small island was dead ahead, its white beaches gleaming. "Pretty sure you need to steer clear of that," Mako said.

Storm didn't respond, but glared at him and turned a few degrees to port. Mako found the spiral-bound book in the chart table and opened it to the section on Jost Van Dyke and Tobago. Instead of reading about the moorings, he concentrated on the nightlife. "Great Harbor looks good."

"If I remember, that's where the customs dock is, and there's plenty of room for a yacht of that size too," Storm said.

They passed Sand Cay and saw masts to starboard. "That must be Little Harbor," Mako said after consulting the chart. Its narrow entrance looked intimidating, and he doubted the larger vessel would try it.

They passed a rocky point, and Storm cut the wheel to starboard. Great Harbor lay ahead, and tied up to a long dock on the far side was the yacht.

"That's the customs dock they're on," Storm said.

Mako looked at his phone. "After five. I guess they're stuck here until tomorrow," he said, relishing the thought of going ashore and freeing himself from Storm. The harbor was busy, home to several popular establishments Mako had read about. He searched the shore for two of the bars in particular: Corsair's, where Hillary had instructed him to leave a message on the walls, and Foxy's were on top of his list.

"Can we find a mooring ball first?" Storm demanded.

After a brief squabble, they were tied up to one of the few remaining moorings, and Mako stood on the bow surveying the scene. Twilight was upon the harbor, and the party was just starting. "I'll take the dinghy and run over to the marina to pay for the mooring," Mako offered after changing.

"I'll ride over with you and watch the yacht while you do whatever it is you do."

That was good enough for Mako, and he climbed from the swim platform into the dinghy, careful to wipe the salt spray from the seat. Storm closed the cabin and joined him. Silently they rode through the mooring field, each contemplating their own missions. Storm eased the dinghy to the dock by Foxy's, and Mako hopped out.

Mako started bopping to the reggae music coming from the bar the second Storm dropped him off. He deftly avoided a group of island children dressed in Catholic school uniforms looking for handouts, and ran directly in to the harbormaster.

"That'll be twenty dollars for the mooring," the man said.

Mako dug in his pockets and pulled out the requisite bill. "That yacht over there." He pointed to the large dock. "Seen anyone come off her?" he asked.

The man looked him over, and Mako pulled out a five-dollar bill. Before he could offer it, the man's agile fingers reached out and snatched it from his grip, the bill quickly disappearing into his pocket. "A young lady was by earlier." He gave Mako the look again.

Mako was having none of it. "Where'd she go?"

He shook his head and turned away. “It’s a small town. You’ll find her.”

Mako brushed off the insult and strode down the dock to the sandy road that ran along the beach. The music came from a purple-and-green building on the right. *Must be Foxy's*, he thought and headed toward the entrance. The bar was open to the night air and about three-quarters full. Local bartenders poured rum drinks which the deeply tanned tourists drank while swaying to the music. He cruised through the room, stopping at the corner of the bar near a stage where a band was playing. Several people were dancing, but the woman was not here. He thought about having a drink and waiting, but his stomach was growling and he had planned on checking out Corsair’s. Like the harbormaster had said, it was a small island—he would find her.

He headed down the road, having to dodge several local vehicles cruising the narrow street. After passing a handful of quieter restaurants, bars and gift shops, he found Corsair’s on the right. The colorful building had a Jimmy Buffet song coming from its open bar and dining room. Several couples were at long high-top tables out front, watching the boats bobbing on the moon-dappled water. He moved slowly past the crowded dining area, the smell of the food tempting him, but the bar was just ahead, and he froze when he saw her.

She was by herself at the small bar, sipping what looked like straight tequila. In a perfect world, he would have found a spot and watched her, to see if she was really alone and take the mood of the place, but the bar was less than a dozen seats, flanked by a fish-fighting chair off a charter boat. He took the straight-on approach.

“Well, hey there. From the other night, right?” he said, as if she didn’t think he would remember. In many places he could be accused of stalking, but cruisers circumnavigated the islands, often stopping at each to sample the bars and food. It was not uncommon to run into someone on more than one island.

"Mako, was it?" she answered and slid over a seat. "Join me?"

He wasted no time and sat next to her, wondering if he had ever told her his name. "I'm kind of hungry, mind if we skip right to dinner?" he asked.

"Suits me," she said and looked to the dining room, catching the eye of a waiter who showed them to an empty table by the road.

Mako looked around at the notes scrawled in marker all over the walls and ceiling, left by tourists over the years. He thought about what Hillary had said, but he needed to concentrate on the task at hand. They ordered, and Mako enjoyed the best seafood in the islands.

"You were hungry," she said.

He finished the bowl of fish stew, soaking up the last of the sauce with a piece of bread. "Sorry. Didn't do such a good job provisioning the boat."

"Guess you need a woman's touch," she laughed and finished her fish. "If you'll excuse me for a minute." She got up, grabbed her phone from the tabletop and left in the direction of the bathroom.

Normally he would want to get her alone, but that was crossing a fine line between work and play. Besides, the sailboat was off-limits with Storm there, and the Iranian was on the yacht. The best he could do was to get as much information from her as he could. He sat back when she returned.

"Nightcap?" she asked.

He smiled, got up and held her chair, enjoying her touch as she brushed against him. Mako signaled the waiter and left the company credit card on the table. Alicia was going to love this one, he thought as they entered the bar and found two stools.

"Absinthe?" he asked the bartender. The decorative bottles holding red, green and yellow liquor had grabbed his eye.

"Name's Vinny." The man behind the bar looked like a pirate, with his grey-streaked hair tied back in a ponytail. With his gold earrings and multiple tattoos, he looked like the corsair the island was named after, until he spoke and his New Jersey accent belied him. "Slide back in the fighting chair and I'll give you a taste."

Mei Lan poked him in the ribs, urging him on. "I'll do it if you do it," he said as he got into the chair and leaned back. With his feet on the platform, he closed his eyes, opened his mouth and braced himself as the sting of the liquor hit his tongue. Vinny poured a heavy shot, stopping to allow him to swallow. The liquor was harsh, tasting of licorice, but sugary at the same time.

He opened his eyes, ready to trade places with the girl, when he saw the gun pointed at his head.

CHAPTER 14

"Sorry 'bout this, Vinny," the waiter said, the barrel of the gun shaking, but still pointed at Mako's head.

"Shit, man. What the hell?" Vinny asked, his thick accent a stark contrast to the waiter's local dialect.

The gun swung momentarily in toward the bar. Vinny ducked, and the waiter turned it back to Mako. He looked at Mei Lan, who dropped her eyes, and he knew he had been set up.

"Okay, now," the waiter said and turned to the bar. "Everybody chill." He looked at Vinny. "Toss me the keys to the jeep."

Mako watched the exchange, looking for a way out.

From behind the bar he heard Vinny. "Not the company truck, man."

The waiter reached over the bar and extended his free hand. "Do as I say. I gotta do this for my family. You know my mom's sick. You've been good to me. I'll bring it back."

Vinny reached into his pocket and handed him a set of keys. "Do the right thing. It's not too late," he pleaded.

"Okay. Please be a good man and don't give me no trouble," the waiter said, turning back to the fighting chair and pointing the gun back at Mako. With the barrel, he motioned through the open bar to the beach across the street, where an old truck that looked like a cross between an army jeep and a pickup was parked.

Mako knew he was out of time. This was not the waiter's game, and he took advantage of his nervousness. Slowly he pushed his body up, leaning out of the chair, but instead of rising, he lunged forward and head-butted the waiter. Both men went down immediately, crashing against a table and knocking its contents onto the floor. Before he could recover, a foot landed in the small of his back. The gun was several feet away, and he swept his legs around in a low sweep kick, trying to stop Mei Lan. She reached for the gun, but the kick landed and knocked her to the floor. The waiter was moving now, and Mako knew he would have to act quickly. He looked up and saw another kick coming toward his head and ducked. The blow landed near his temple, and his head bounced off of the concrete floor. Another kick hit his kidney, and he rolled into a fetal position to protect himself. With his head ringing, he looked around for a way out and saw the marker on the floor.

In that instant, Mako remembered what Hillary had said. It may have been a joke then, but now it might be the only way to save himself. He extended a hand and reached for the marker.

"Get the truck," Mei Lan called out.

Mako knew this was his only chance and turned to the wall as if to use it for protection. He looked back at Mei Lan, but she was watching the waiter back the truck up. In the seconds he had before she turned back, he scrawled *Mako's on Shahansha*. Right before she grabbed him, he pulled his phone out of his pocket and slid it under a fallen menu. And then he felt the cold steel of the gun's barrel touch his forehead.

"Slowly, now. Get in," she said.

Mako climbed into the bed of the truck and felt the old shocks complain as the waiter crawled in beside him. Someone got in the cab and he heard the engine start. The gears ground as the driver, who he suspected was Mei Lan, fumbled with the manual transmission. Finally she found reverse and the truck lurched backwards, almost stalling before he felt the clutch engage and then heard a metal-on-metal sound as she searched for first gear. With a jolt, they were underway, his body slamming against the hard bed of the truck with every pothole in the sandy road. After a few minutes, the road turned to asphalt and their speed increased. They wound up a hill, made a hard left and started descending. Minutes later, they came to a stop with a squeal of the brakes.

Two crewmen stood there waiting. They approached and unceremoniously dragged him from the bed of the truck and onto the yacht. The customs office was closed until the morning, and there was no one around,. No one to hear if he screamed or help him if he ran. All the action of the small town was focused on the bars. With enough resistance to let them know he was not a pushover, he was pulled up the ramp to midship, where they let him fall onto the deck.

"Well. We have Mako Storm as our guest," Mei Li said, laughing as if she had told a joke only she understood. "Lock him up. I'll deal with him later."

Mako was hauled across the fiberglass deck, through a door and down several flights of stairs before being deposited in an empty cabin adjacent to what he guessed was the engine room. The rumble of the generators next door precluded any attempt at yelling for help. The door slammed, and he heard the lock engage.

***

* * *

John Storm watched the entire incident from his hiding spot behind the restaurant, but without a firearm he was helpless. The fool of a boy and his penchant for women had gotten him in trouble again, he thought. Although he couldn't follow the truck on foot, he had watched its headlights, unsure whether he was concerned or relieved when he saw the jeep turn down the hill and descend toward the yacht. But a known, no matter how bad, was always better than an unknown. Now he needed to figure out how to handle this new development.

He was across the street from Corsair's when he saw the headlights of the truck return, its wide wheel base and loud engine making it easy to spot from a distance. As it approached, he ran across to the beach and ducked down behind a small boat pulled up onto the sand. The driver got out, and Storm could tell by his body language that he was nervous. Slowly, he walked across the street to the restaurant with his head down and his hands in his pockets. He looked unarmed. Storm rose and followed.

"Easy, Vinny. Man, I had no choice," the waiter pleaded.

"Okay, kid, calm down. But goddamn," Vinny's accented voice came from behind the bar.

Storm walked into the empty restaurant and saw the two men, the bar the only barrier between them.

"You the man, Vinny. Best boss on the island. I would never hurt you. You gotta know that," the waiter sobbed. "I just did it for my mom."

Storm watched Vinny as he poured a shot and downed it. He paused for a second and poured another for himself, then reached for another glass and filled it, sliding it across the bar to the waiter. "Let it go. We all got crosses to bear."

While the two men drank, Storm looked around the room.

"Looks like you had some action here. Cruisers and alcohol, huh?" Storm said and righted the overturned table.

"If you only knew, man," Vinny said. "You don't need to do that."

"No trouble," Storm said. He picked up the menus and noticed the cell phone. With his back turned to the bar, he bent over and picked it up, holding it as if it were his own.

"Best of luck to you. Guess they shut you down for the night," Storm said. "Think I'll go over to Foxy's."

"Gotta think outside the Fox, man," Vinny said.

He had no intention of going to Foxy's. Instead, Storm walked the beach road acting like a drunken tourist, pausing every few feet to look at a store or gaze out to sea. In reality, he was checking for a tail. He continued past Foxy's for a quarter mile on the deserted street and decided he was alone. Backtracking, he took to the water, and waded around the piles beneath the bar's deck. He made his way to the far side of the dinghy dock and slid over the side of the inflatable. Peering over the low gunwales, he watched for another few minutes before starting the engine and heading back to the sailboat. With the other boats as cover, the mooring was the best place to keep an eye on the yacht.

Once on deck, he secured the dinghy and sat in the cockpit watching the water. Other dinghies shuttled people from ship to shore and back, while kids swam off the sterns of a few catamarans. Several minutes later, he went below and turned a light on. He pulled Mako's phone from his pocket and set it on the table in front of him. Without the skills to analyze it, he did what he could, checking the email, text messages, and voicemail. The boy was careless, he thought as he read the emails and texts from Alicia.

After absorbing everything he could, he thought about what to do next. He knew from the messages that Mako had told her of their partnership, so he saw no harm in checking in. Back in the phone screen, he hit her contact information and pressed the phone symbol next to her mobile number. A thousand miles away, the phone rang and he waited.

***

"Where have you been?" she asked.

"I'm not the boy," a strange voice said.

She closed her eyes and thought for a second as the voice ran through the database in her head. "Storm? Is that you?"

"Yeah. They've got Mako."

She suspected something bad had happened after not hearing from him. "Explain," she said, and listened carefully as Storm recounted the abduction. She was about to ask how he could let that happen when she realized that if he had interfered, they might both be dead. "You know the Agency's not paying for this," she said.

"So I heard, but there won't be an Agency if we don't stop them."

Her email icon popped up with a new message. "Gotta go. Hold on to the phone and I'll call you back."

She opened the email screen and saw the address as coming from Lloyd's of London. Wondering if she had overreacted and it was just an ad, she looked at the message. When she saw the attached picture of Mako dropping from the air-conditioning duct, her heart caught in her throat. Switching off the communications with Cody to run the dive charter had caused her to make a rookie mistake—she had never shut off the security cameras. Hoping this was not as bad as it looked, she scanned the message. There was only a name and phone number that said to call anytime.

It was almost midnight Eastern time, and though it was five a.m. in London, she opened her encrypted voice over Internet program and entered the number. Seconds later it was answered.

"Thank you for calling so quickly," a woman's voice said.

Alicia was silent for a moment, and she continued, "My name is Valerie, and I am head of security here at Lloyd's. It seems that someone reporting to you had an incident here last Saturday."

The woman knew enough. "Is this line encrypted on your end?" Alicia asked.

"Yes," she answered. "Your agent took some data off our system."

There was no point in denying it. "Yes. It is a matter of national security."

"For us as well. Does your government think we are so greedy that we would help the Iranians?"

"Well, no," she stuttered. This was way over her pay grade. "We were working on a contract. I do not make the decisions as to what the missions are and why. We only execute them," Alicia said.

"Maybe we can agree that both our intelligence agencies are not very intelligent," Valerie said.

Alicia was getting anxious about Mako and had no idea where this was leading. "What can I do for you?"

"Lloyd's is willing to triple your contract for retrieval of the encryption code."

Alicia sat up in her chair. This was a lot of money. "Go on."

"Do you have the data?"

She hesitated. "It was lost in the Thames."

After a long pregnant pause, the woman continued. “The encryption code on that drive held the key to Nitro Zeus. Have you heard of the operation?”

Before she answered, she opened a secure window and typed in the name. The screen, linked to a back door in the Agency’s database, showed the program. “Of course,” she answered, while reading as fast as she could. The summary said enough, and she knew how valuable the data was. In the event that Iran continued to enrich uranium in the pursuit of a nuclear weapon, the operation would go into effect. The country would be shut down: air traffic, radar, power grid. They would be helpless. What she didn’t tell the agent on the other end of the line was that if her theory was correct, with the two cases of enriched uranium brought by the Chinese, the operation wouldn’t be launched until after a nuclear attack had happened.

“Somehow Cyrus got the encryption code and contracted us to place it on our computers for safekeeping.”

“But why…?”

“Because we didn’t know. It was to be simply an encryption code. We pride ourselves on having the most secure network on earth. The Swiss bank of data, if you will. Which was why you had to place an agent in our building to manually transfer it instead of hacking in from a distance. We have to give you credit for getting that far—no one else, not even our best in-house hackers, has been able to do what you did.”

“Then if the code is missing, aren’t the Iranians powerless?” Alicia asked.

“If only things were so easy.”

CHAPTER 15

Storm stared at the phone, waiting for it to ring or whatever it did. After a few minutes of silence, he grabbed the field glasses from the chart table and took the phone on deck with him. The harbor had quieted down, not for the night, but the kids had gone to bed and most of the boats were dark now. Foxy's was still going strong, the bass beat audible throughout the mooring field, and there was a trickle of dinghy traffic to and from the club. That would go on for a while, he thought, and trained the glasses on the yacht.

A few lights were still on, mostly around the bridge area, and he suspected most of the activity would be going on below. He watched patiently until he had identified the guards and memorized their movements. There were two men patrolling the deck. From this distance, he could not see any visible weapons, but he had no doubt the men were well armed. Extrapolating a watch schedule, he guessed that there would be six guards aboard. Whether they did double duty as crewmen, he didn't know.

***

Alicia thought about what she had just heard and texted Cody, even though he was only two doors away. He came in bleary-eyed, obviously having just woken up. He stood behind her, and she gave him a few minutes to get his bearings and absorb what was on the screen.

"Shit."

"Yeah, and I'll triple it, which is what Lloyd's just offered to do to our contract if we can retrieve the information."

He rubbed his eyes and went to the adjacent desk. "Shit. Does the Agency know?" Cody asked. He cracked his knuckles and started typing.

"They know what we knew, that Cyrus was storing the encryption data for Nitro Zeus on Lloyd's drives. We're private contractors. I don't see the harm in working both ends."

Cody went to his captain's chair and started working furiously on something. After a few minutes, they both glanced at each other and spoke at the same time. "Go first," Alicia said.

"It looks like Cyrus was in China before London. The agreement was that the Iranians remove their weapons-grade uranium from their country. I'm guessing they let the inspectors see it shipped to China, but China has no inspectors, and with a bit of subterfuge and a long route around the world through the BVI—now it's on the way back. With the code to stop Nitro Zeus and what looks like a hundred pounds of top-shelf uranium, Cyrus can walk into Tehran and ask for the keys to the bus. If they don't buy it, he leaves the uranium, tells the US what happened and lets them run their operation, effectively putting the country back in the Stone Age." He sat back, staring at the screen.

She told him what she had figured out. "Cyrus. Shahansha—King of Kings. He wants to jumpstart the old Persian empire."

"I'm not getting Lloyd's interest," he said.

"It took me a while, but this could ruin them. If word gets out that Cyrus was using them to store the data, they would lose face on two fronts. First, though it's not well known, they are insuring data through what their own chief of security just told me is the safest network in the world. If word gets out about that we were able to penetrate their security, even though we lost the data, their reputation is destroyed. Second, if this comes out that they enabled Cyrus to stop Nitro Zeus from their headquarters in London, then they have compromised world security. There is no happy ending for them unless we get the data back and they turn it in to British intelligence."

"And you're betting that Cyrus has a backup."

"Wouldn't you?" She opened a VOIP screen again and dialed Mako's number. "We need to bring Storm in as a partner."

"Shit," Cody said.

***

Storm heard the phone vibrate on the table in the galley and stepped down to the cabin, instinctively covering the screen to hide its light in case anyone was watching, but the party around him was still going on and he could have started a disco ball and remained unnoticed.

"Yeah," he said and listened as Alicia explained the situation and her theory about the cases and Cyrus's plan.

"One-third?" he asked. "That's the same deal that I have with the Agency."

"You think you can do this on your own?"

He thought about that for a second and realized she was right. He would need help. Knowing her by reputation was one thing, but seeing her operate and piece together both Cyrus's plot and the deal with Lloyd's in the half hour since they had last talked was impressive.

"Okay. I'm in."

"And one more thing." She explained her theory of what the two cases contained. "We need to verify their contents."

"And how do you suppose we do that?" he asked.

"I'm working on it. For now, let's see what we can do about Mako. Can you get close to the yacht and take some video? I can't get anything from a satellite until daylight."

Storm looked out the small window. There was enough dinghy traffic that he could blend in. "Sure. But you better tell me how to use this thing."

Alicia turned him over to Cody, who walked him through the basics, ending with a warning not to get it wet. He laughed. This was almost as good as a CIA operation, and he wished that Q, the quartermaster in the James Bond movies with all the great toys, actually existed. Turning to the galley, he searched the drawers until he found a plastic bag. He placed the phone in it, doing his best to seal it, and stuck it in his pocket. After changing into dark clothes, he thought about reaching into the engine compartment for some oil to soot his face, but decided that would be too obvious in the crowded harbor. One flashlight pointed randomly at him would blow his cover. Before he left, he searched through the kitchen drawers and found the knives, selecting two that might work. He slid the paring knife into his shoe, making sure the sock shielded the blade, and looked around for anything else that might serve as a weapon. The orange emergency case caught his eye, and he removed the flare gun and two extra flares.

Using the cover of the moored boats, he wove his way through the harbor in a seemingly random pattern, slowly working toward the customs dock, where the ship was tied up. He thought about the plot Alicia had laid out as he closed in on the yacht, but several things didn't add up. What was Mei Li's involvement, and why was her daughter with her? And why here?

The Chinese women's presence could be easily explained if China was in fact sponsoring Cyrus's plan. That made sense. He would need a powerful ally, and China needed Iran's oil. The other question vexed him, and he had to put it out of his mind as he neared the *Shahansha*. Leaving the phone in the baggie, he fumbled through the screens to the camera and started the video. With one hand on the camera and the other on the steering handle extending from the engine, he closed on the yacht, trying to look like a tourist. He was within a dozen feet of the ship when he heard a guard above him yell to move away. He waved back and turned back to the harbor.

Mission over, he headed back to the sailboat. Once he was back on board, he called Alicia, who handed him off to Cody. With the speaker on, he followed the instructions to upload the video and asked to speak to Alicia. He wanted his questions answered.

"We need to find out where they are headed. The ship's at the customs dock, and I suspect they will clear out as soon as they open in the morning. We need to get Mako out now."

Before she could respond, he heard a boat approach, larger than a dinghy by the sound of the motor. He stuck his head out of the cabin and saw the twin-engine outboard coast to a stop. It drifted close enough for him to see the outline of a woman standing in the bow.

"Permission to come aboard?" she asked.

Storm was not sure who she was or what to do. "I think you've got the wrong boat," he said, trying to discourage her.

"No. The *Escape Yourself.* Right boat. Wrong guy, maybe. Where's Mako?"

He should have known, but that didn't help. Without waiting for permission, she motioned the driver forward and jumped from bow to bow. Storm watched her nimbly hop between boats and make her way back to the cockpit.

"I talked to Vinny and saw the note on the wall of Corsair's. Is he in trouble?" she asked.

"And who are you?"

"Hillary," she said, and extended a hand.

He shook it and looked her in the eye. This was not Mako's typical barfly kind of girl, he thought. "Maybe we should talk," he said. "I'd offer you something, but all that idiot stocked up on is booze and Cheetos."

"Never mind that. I could tell there had been a fight in the bar, and Vinny's drinking himself into some kind of stupor. I did get the story from him and saw where Mako scrawled something on the wall." She took a cocktail napkin out of her pocket. "Shahansha? What does that mean?"

Storm figured he might as well play along. "*Shahansha.*" He pointed over to the yacht. "He's being held there."

"What kind of business are you guys in? I'm just a pilot looking for a few days of fun."

He suspected there was more to her than that. "Where'd you learn to fly?"

"Navy, why?" she asked.

After years of running agents, he could tell talent when he saw it. "Don't suppose you'd care to help save the world?"

She gave him a look and smiled. "Been a little bored lately. Whatever."

John found a bottle of water mixed in with all the alcohol in the galley and handed it to her. She sat across from him and drank as he explained their predicament.

"So you guys are CIA? Never would have known it from Mako."

Storm shook his head. "Point taken," he said.

"Maybe it's just a good cover," she said.

He could never figure out how Mako did it. He directed the conversation back to the present. "My concern is that if the yacht gets into open water—and it's wide open out there"—he looked toward the mouth of the harbor—"we wouldn't have a chance of following in this boat, and satellites can only cover so much ground. Their transponders been on so far, but they've been playing by the rules, and you'd expect that. Once they clear customs, the rules change."

"Then we disable him and he's stuck here."

He knew he had seen something behind those eyes. "Exactly. The local marine store, if they even have one here, wouldn't stock parts for that thing."

She finished her water and looked at him. "What are you asking me to do, exactly?"

That was a big unknown, but he figured he would take it a step at a time. "You get uncomfortable and you're out—no questions asked." She nodded and he continued. "I've been watching her for an hour now. There are two guards on deck and probably several more armed crew out of sight. I would assume they are well trained—special forces level, from the importance of what he has on board. And don't forget the women. Mei Li is a known factor and extremely dangerous. Her daughter Mei Lan is an unknown, but I would expect the apple doesn't fall far from the tree."

“Sounds like we’re up against it.”

“As far as boarding—yes. My idea is to get in the water and disable her from underneath, maybe something to the propeller or shaft.”

“I’m not very good in the water. Most of my time is spent well above it,” she said.

“I can handle that part. Just need some gear and tools.” He looked toward shore, wondering what he could round up. “Want another water?” he asked as he went below for the cruising guide.

“Maybe something a little stronger—for the nerves, if you’ve got it.”

He was surprised but brought her a small glass of rum. She took it, but set it down without touching it. He liked that in a partner. They huddled around the small light built into the table and studied the guide. Jost Van Dyke had much to offer in the way of bars, but not much for services.

“That’s a cute dive shop,” she said.

He would have totally missed it. The picture showed a shack on the beach with sign posts and stuff. “That’s where we start.”

She tossed the rum overboard. “Ready.”

***

Mako leaned against the steel bulkhead. They were not taking any chances and had tied his hands and feet with a tether attached to a bolt in the wall, its length barely long enough to allow him to sit. Squatting in total darkness, insulated from even the repetitive slapping of the small waves against the hull—it was sensory deprivation at its finest. He had lost track of time. The bindings cut his wrists whenever he moved and jerked him awake whenever he tried to sleep. With nothing else to do, he stared into the darkness, wondering who was out there and what they were doing.

Storm would be watching, and knowing the old man, he had seen everything. That was good. Alicia was probably clueless, though, her skills unable to penetrate the steel hull surrounding him. He was dressed for a night of partying, not captivity. He didn't even have a belt to hang himself with.

Settling for an awkward position against the wall, he prepared to wait out his destiny. Bored, he kicked off his flip-flops and remembered the bottle opener built into them. Encouraged, he used his feet to slide the sandal close enough to reach. He twisted and grabbed it with both hands, turning it over. The rubber bottom of the right sandal had a small molded cavity in it that held a bottle opener.

Bringing the flip flop to his mouth, he dug into the rubber with his teeth. He spat out small pieces as they came off, and finally he felt the metal loosen. He worked it back and forth until it came free. He dropped the sandal and took the small metal piece from his mouth. It wouldn't do as a weapon, but he had another idea.

CHAPTER 16

Storm followed the shore, looking for an inconspicuous place to beach the dinghy. He wanted to avoid the busier docks toward the right side of the town, still crowded with partiers, and land near the dive shop. Motoring slowly toward the west, he saw the small storefront across the street and looked around, deciding on a spot between two larger boats pulled onto the beach which would provide cover. There were small waves breaking, not enough to cause any worry of swamping, but if he could catch the right one, they could surf the dinghy high onto the beach and avoid having to pull it out of the water. He steered for the opening between the boats.

Timing the wave, he gunned the throttle. The engine responded with a cough and then accelerated. The small boat crested the wave, and he backed off the power. At just the right second, he pulled the dead man's key, lifted the locking pin and swung the engine from the water, raising the propeller before it struck sand.

"Well done," Hillary said and jumped from the still-moving boat. She grabbed the painter and pulled. The wave receded, and the dinghy sat high and dry, well above the tide mark.

Storm joined her on the beach and they walked to the sandy road, looking both ways for anyone that might identify them later.

This far from the bars, the street was quiet. They crossed and hurried to the cover of the dive shop. The area around the small building was illuminated by several spotlights, allowing them to see. They looked into the windows of the shop and saw only merchandise. There was nowhere for a compressor or storage for rental gear. He looked around and saw a small barn-like building behind the shop. That had to be it. He nodded to Hillary and put his fingers to his eyes, telling her to wait and watch.

The area around the barn was thick with low palm trees, and he did his best to stumble through the brush without making noise. Stopping every few seconds, he couldn't see anyone taking an interest. With this terrain, they would have to be well hidden to see him. Staying low, he crossed the small open area to the shed and slid across the front of the building to the door. The padlock was a good sign that he had guessed correctly, and he looked around for another way in. Around the side he found a window. On his tiptoes, he slid it open and hoisted himself over the sill. The shop was dark and he didn't want to risk a light. It was common in the islands for owners or managers to live on premises—any light or sound might bring an investigation.

He searched in the dark, easily finding the tanks. They were in two groups, one with tape over the O ring at the valve, indicating the tank was full, and another without—the empty ones. Grabbing a full tank, he carried it to the window and carefully lifted it through the hole. It dropped soundlessly to the sand. A buoyancy compensator vest, regulator and weight belt followed, and then he swung up and through the opening. With the BC on his back and the regulator around his neck, he walked across the road to where the dinghy was beached, carrying the tank in his arms like a baby.

Hillary met him there, and with the gear aboard, they swung the dinghy bow to the water and pulled it into the surf. The weight of the tank and gear in the bow made their hurried exit from the beach less graceful than their entry. Clear of the swells, Storm jerked the cord to start the motor. It coughed and died as a large swell lifted the small boat, threatening to toss it back onto the beach. He pulled again, and this time the motor started. Storm sped towards the customs dock while Hillary bailed the water that had come over the bow.

The dinghy bounced over the waves, taking on water with each one, finally reaching the calmer water beyond the beach. He slowed a hundred yards from the yacht and steered closer to the pier. It was substantial, built by the government, not the local bar owners, and had plenty of clearance underneath. The sound from the engine echoed. Storm shut off the motor and grabbed the two oars.

"I got that. You get ready," Hillary said and set the oars into the locks. She adjusted herself and started to row slowly towards the shadow cast by the yacht's hull.

***

Mako heard someone outside the door and contorted his body enough to stuff the metal bottle opener in his pocket. The mess on the floor was another matter, and he used his bound legs to sweep it toward his body in an effort to conceal it. Just as he finished, the door opened and the overhead light came on, temporarily blinding him. Squinting into the light, he saw two figures but was unable to identify them.

"You will tell us what you and that traitorous woman know," the voice said.

He thought he could identify the voice, but his eyes were still adjusting to the light. "What are you talking about?" he said—his stock answer to just about any question about anything.

A bare foot kicked him and he looked to its source. His eyes had adjusted now, and he saw Mei Lan standing over him with her mother at her side. She wound up for another kick, and he did his best to curl into a fetal position to protect himself.

"Stop," the older woman called out. "You need to learn when force is effective. All that partying and playing you do clouds your judgment. First you try and seduce him, now you want to hurt him."

Mei Lan moved away. Her mother stood in front of Mako. "You see, I am your friend, yes?"

The interchange between the women would have been entertaining if not for his predicament. Mako nodded. He would do anything rather than suffer the man-hating kicks delivered by her daughter.

"Mako, that's correct?" she asked.

"Yes."

"Very good. This is progress." She looked at her daughter as if to teach her a lesson. "This woman. Alicia Phon." She said the last name with disdain. "You work with her?"

Mako looked around. She should already know the answers to these questions. He wondered if she was probing now, and how much she actually knew. "Who?" he asked.

Mother turned to daughter and nodded her head. The spin kick came so quickly he didn't have a chance to react, and his body crumpled when the side of her callused foot struck his temple. The rope tethering him to the bulkhead was the only thing that kept him upright. Mei Lan glared at him, ready to strike again.

"Now, should I leave you two lovebirds alone, or do you want Mama to chaperone?" she asked.

Mako couldn't believe the change in the younger woman. From flirting and dancing with her the other night to stone-cold jujitsu man-hating machine. "I work with her," he confirmed. If he had to talk, he would dish out the information piecemeal, hopefully giving Storm or Alicia time to do something.

"And you are under contract with the CIA?"

"Yes."

"To what end?" she asked.

He paused for a second, wondering if she was simply looking out for herself and her daughter or if this was really about the contract. "It is to recover the encryption code that Cyrus placed on Lloyd's computers."

"That is all?" she asked.

He had been right. "There was nothing about you two."

"Time will tell if you are lying or not." She turned and left the cabin, looking back at Mei Lan.

The younger woman stared at him with pure evil in her eyes, and he knew at some point, and probably soon, he would have to face her. Mei Li gave her a look and she followed. The door slammed behind them, and he was almost relieved as the locks engaged.

***

The darkness under the pier enveloped them. Storm had some dive experience but was by no means an expert. He fumbled assembling the gear, and when he finally got in the water, he was unable to find the air vent on the BC. The trapped air forced him right back to the surface, and he floundered there, losing his regulator in the process. Clinging to the dinghy, he caught his breath. "This isn't going to work."

"Maybe we should come back in the morning, when it's light?"

"If we can see them, they can see us." He eased out of the gear and climbed back onto the dinghy. "We need to figure another way to get aboard," he said. He watched her as she pulled on the oars, bringing them out of the cover of the pier. Looking at her, he had an idea. "You have your uniform on the sailboat?" he asked.

"Yes, but…."

"Well, I won't fit in it. Unless you have a better idea."

She paused for a minute. "We need to get out of here anyway. Give me a few minutes to think about this."

He stowed the gear and started the engine. She would have to make her own decision. The small outboard purred behind them as he made his way back through the mooring field and found the boat. They boarded, leaving the gear in the dinghy. He laid out his plan, and they sat silently across from each other in the dark cockpit.

Finally she spoke. "If there's no other way."

"I can't think of anything. You board like you belong there. Tell the guards you're a pilot on standby in case the helicopter is needed," he started to explain.

"Just like that. With my Cape Air uniform?"

"This lot doesn't fly commercial. They'll just see the uniform," he explained, knowing her looks wouldn't hurt either.

"And what do I do?" she asked.

"Have them take you to the top deck where the helipad is to do a preflight. Take your time. Have some coffee, relax."

"Right. That'll be very relaxing. And where will you be?"

He hadn't worked out all the details yet. "One, maybe two of the guards will be with you. I can take the other out if necessary and find the engine room. There should only be three on duty now. I'll disable her from there and hopefully find Mako in the process." It sounded good, but he would need help to disable the ship.

"When?" she asked.

"Dawn. The principals should be asleep." From what he knew after watching the ship for several days, Cyrus and Mei Li wouldn't rise until after eight.

"And how do I get off?"

"I'll text you when I'm done. Make a show of it. Tell them the chopper is good to go and you're going to town to get some breakfast."

"It can't be that easy," she said.

He knew she was right. The best-laid plans always changed as soon as the opposition reacted. "Why don't you try and get some sleep? Take the forward berth. I'll wake you."

She left the cockpit and disappeared below. Storm picked up the phone and rolled it in his hand. It was close to midnight, and he hesitated before he dialed, but knew he would need Alicia once he got into the engine room.

***

Alicia was near frantic as she watched the screen. An advisory from the NSA had just been passed to Homeland Security warning the directors to be ready to implement Nitro Zeus. There were few details, but the memo was clear. Iran had threatened a nuclear attack against Israel. She went deep into the Agency's database, searching information well beyond her reach as a contractor, looking for anything that could clarify the situation. It took her a few minutes, but she found it.

An interagency memo had been released two days ago about the loss of the encryption data. There was nothing that said what the contract was, only that it had failed and another contractor was involved now. She cross-referenced her own contract against the Agency's computer and found the smoking gun. An email between two workers had been sent before the original contract terms had been agreed. In a breach of security, the details of the contract were revealed, explicitly stating the data was to be placed on Lloyd's network.

The pieces fell into place from here. Just days after the initial email, someone had hacked the CIA. All signs pointed to the Chinese flexing their newly found cyber-muscle. That might be another reason why Mei Li and her daughter were with the Iranian. The Chinese, desperately in need of oil and tired of dealing with the theocracy, wanted a simpler solution, and that was Cyrus.

"Cody," she yelled across the room, but he was oblivious, deeply ensconced in the command chair with his headphones on. Instead of yelling again, she texted him.

He removed the headphones and laughed. "Sorry, got a little wrapped up there."

"You need to have a look at this. Mako and Storm are off the grid, and we have a bigger problem." While she waited for him to review the information on the screen, she opened her secret weapon, the same system that had identified Mei Li on the *Shahansha.* The screen started to populate, and she entered several strings of code to filter the information, specifically limiting the search to Iran, China and the British Virgin Islands. The lines started moving around, and she was left with a trail of communication that was undeniable.

* * *

***

"Sorry if I woke you, but I need your help," Storm started.

"No sleep here. I was just going to contact you."

There was a pause on the line, both waiting for the other to speak. "I have a plan to get on the yacht in the morning and disable it. We can't let it leave the dock or we'll lose him." Storm laid out his plan.

"I agree, a delay would benefit us," she said.

"Care to fill me in?" Storm asked.

"He needs to get those cases to Iran. The NSA just put an alert out. The trip, even on the yacht, is almost ten thousand miles and they would be vulnerable going through the Straits of Gibraltar and then the Suez Canal. The timeline is now. I suspect he's going to have to fly." She had done the math. At forty knots they would make almost a thousand miles per day. Best case it would take ten days of nonstop sailing to reach Iran. It might have been the plan before the alert, but the window of opportunity was now closed.

"If it were me, I'd find the closest banana republic and hop a plane. Better to just stop him here," he said.

"Agreed. How can I help you, then?" she asked.

"I have a plan to get aboard at dawn and disable the ship from the engine room. I'll need the fastest way to do the most damage."

She was silent for a minute. "Just pulling up the specs." She paused again.

Storm watched the now-quiet harbor while he waited. A sole dinghy was cruising from ship to ship, lost, trying to find their own. There were still a few lights aboard *Shahansha*. In the dim light, he studied the ship, memorizing the deck layout.

"Okay. The engine room is mostly computer-driven. This should be a piece of cake."

He disconnected, thinking what was easy for her might be a little more of a challenge for him, but without her help he'd have no choice but to take a sledgehammer to the equipment. If this went as planned, they would never know what hit them. There was one other loose end, and he texted Alicia back, asking for a deck layout. Once the ship was disabled, he would have to find Mako.

Unable to sleep, he watched the harbor settle in for the night. There was one last burst of activity when the last dinghies left shore and Foxy's lights went off. Still, he sat there thinking about tomorrow.

CHAPTER 17

The vibration of the phone startled Storm awake. The last thing he remembered was an unsettling dream about Mako. It was still dark, and blinded by the glow of the screen, he had to take a minute to allow his vision to adjust before he could read the message. Alicia must have been up all night, he thought as he followed her directions and opened the two emails, saving the two PDF files to the phone's memory. After thanking her, he opened the documents and worked the screen to zoom in on the different areas. Much preferring paper, he cursed under his breath as the phone didn't obey his commands, but finally he figured out how to manipulate the images. One was the deck layout from the manufacturer. He assumed that Cyrus had customized the yacht, but this would give him a place to start. The second was a layout of the engine room, which read like Greek to him. He hoped there was cell service in the bowels of the ship, knowing he would have to call her when he was in the room for direction.

The sky was still dark when he woke Hillary. A quick review of the galley revealed only alcohol and chips—not even coffee. He grabbed the chips and went back on deck, eating from the bag and studying the deck plan while he waited for her to get ready. It only took her a few minutes, and he held the bag out for her.

"Breakfast?"

"Think I'll pass there," she said and sat down next to him. "What about Mako?" she asked. "Have you heard anything?"

He held the phone between them and showed her the lower deck layout, pointing to two holds. "I'd bet he's in one of those."

"You think he's still alive, then?" she asked.

"No reason not to. This bunch is smart. They'll keep him as long as there is any chance he could be valuable." He saw the relief on her face and wondered if she really did like Mako—and then reprimanded himself for wondering why. Of all the women he had ever seen him with, she was by far the best choice. "Ready when you are."

He dropped down to the dinghy, deciding to leave the dive gear in case they needed it. She followed him, handing her flight case down before boarding. With the flight bag and her uniform, he was sure she would not be questioned. He nodded at her, asking if she was ready, and released the painter.

In the early hour, the buzz of the outboard was the only sound in the harbor, and he kept the speed down so as not to attract attention. The last thing he needed was an upset hungover boater noticing Hillary's uniform. After clearing the mooring field, he headed to shore, hopped out and beached the dinghy, having to do the work himself so she wouldn't get wet. He stripped the toolbox of anything that would fit in his pockets, relieved to find a utility knife that might serve as a weapon. After a quick survey of Hillary, they moved off down the road.

He was not sure how to leave her, if he should hug her or just let her go, so he settled on a pat on the shoulder. She stood by the gangway connecting the yacht to the pier and called for permission to come aboard. Her hail was met a few minutes later by a uniformed crewman. Storm couldn't help but notice the barely concealed gun tucked in the back of his pants. They talked for a minute across the divide before he waved her aboard. *So far, so good*, he thought. Now he had to find the other guard.

That problem handled itself when he came into view at the top of the stairs leading to the helipad. He must have been up there keeping watch on the harbor. Storm had a brief pang of anxiety, hoping that they hadn't noticed her in the dinghy, but after a few minutes, it was apparent that they were flirting with her.

He took his eyes from the top deck and moved to the stern of the yacht, trying to find a blind spot where he would not be seen. After a quick look up, he saw no one watching and vaulted the rail, his knees resisting as he landed in a crouch on the deck. Ignoring the pain, he stood up and immediately went to the hatch, where he opened the dogs securing it. Pulling it towards him, he entered. He looked around, trying to orient himself with the plans that Alicia had sent, and moved down the passageway, finding the stairs exactly where he expected them to be.

Taking the treads two at a time, he reached the landing and swung around the corner, repeating the process until he found himself on the lowest deck. Another watertight hatch blocked the passageway, but it was partially open, and he carefully pushed the steel door. Down in the bowels of the ship, things were not as well maintained as above deck, and the hinges creaked, causing him to freeze in place. He waited, listening intently for any sound. After a minute, he proceeded through another watertight hatch and found himself in the engine room.

The image in his mind of what an engine room should look like was nowhere close to what he saw in front of him. This looked more like pictures he had seen of the Space Station than the engine room on a ship. Racks holding computer equipment lined one wall, while pumps and pipes, set symmetrically and painted in white enamel, lined another. Although it was probably loud when the ship was underway, it was fairly quiet now, with just a generator humming in the background. He closed the door and looked around for a section of loose pipe to lock it with, but the room was immaculate—nothing was out of place. He closed the door and pulled out the phone.

Alicia answered right away. She had him take a quick picture of each wall and send them so she could guide him through the process. Under other circumstances, he would have taken the tools he had and attacked the machinery, but they had agreed this shouldn't look like sabotage. He looked around at the equipment while he waited for Alicia to call back.

"Go to the wall across from the door."

Storm walked across and found himself in front of a supercomputer.

"You need to find the oil pressure control and pull the circuit board out."

He read the tags clearly identifying each component and found what she described. There were several gauges, indicator lights and a handle. The circuit board came free with an easy tug. "Okay."

"Whatever you can do to disable it. Maybe pry loose some of the relays or transistors," she ordered.

Storm reached into his pocket and removed a flat-bladed screwdriver he had taken from the canister on the dinghy. With its tip, he tore into the board and replaced it. "Done. Won't they find out?"

"Damage to the systems we will be working with will only be noticed once they try and get underway," she said impatiently.

"What now?"

"Find the bow thruster controls and do the same. They should be high up toward the right."

He reached for the handle and pulled out the board. After tearing several components free, he replaced it.

"Ready?" she asked, but did not wait for an answer. "Now for the generator controls. Turn to the left. There should be several buttons and gauges. Right next to them you should find a circuit breaker."

He found what she described. "Go ahead."

"Disable the breaker."

He didn't think twice and was about to stick the screwdriver in the space between the two poles of the breaker and pull it apart, but stopped, remembering that part of the mission was to leave no trace. Instead, he pulled out the control board, immediately regretting the decision when an alarm went off and the ship went dark.

"What's happening?" she asked.

"Alarms. Dammit."

"Was it running? I assumed they would be on shore power," she explained.

"Well, we have a problem now," he said and disconnected. He turned to where he thought the door was and, with his hands extended in the pitch-black room, reached for the wall. Moving toward the corner, he found the handle and pushed the door, but it was locked. He tried again and realized that with the generator shut down, the pumps would be disabled as well. Without the pumps, the watertight hatches must have locked automatically. Moving to the opposite corner, where he remembered another door, he stumbled and hit his head on a valve. He was on his knees now and didn't need to feel his head to know he was bleeding. Removing his shirt, he rolled and tied it around his head as a makeshift bandage. Back on his feet, he found the door and turned the handle.

The access to the real engine room opened, and he entered. He couldn't see, but he could tell by the smell of oil and fuel where he was. The room had to have ventilation, and he moved down the narrow corridor between the equipment, banging against hard steel pipes and valves as he went.

He remembered he had Mako's phone and pulled it from his pocket, both to use as a light and for the deck plans Alicia had made him download. The equipment room resembled the picture enough for him to find the ventilation shaft across the room. He climbed onto a large pump and reached for the panel. Just as he was about to remove it, he heard voices. He shut off the light from the phone before it gave him away and put it in his pocket. Trying to be as quiet as possible, he used both hands, working the thumbscrews holding the grate. The last nut came loose and he removed the grille, grabbing for it before it hit the ground and hoisting himself into the shaft just as the beam from a flashlight started scanning the room. Just before it found him, he reached back out and grabbed the grille, pulling it onto the opening seconds before the beam hit it.

The light moved away, and he tried to relax his muscles. If he cramped up in this tight space, things would get ugly. Laid out in the duct, he tried to relax as he listened and waited. Light from a flashlight bled through the bottom of the door. He heard voices and then the whine of a battery-operated drill from the adjacent room. Without warning, the lights came back on and two men burst into the room.

Storm was stuck. If he moved, he would drop the grate and reveal himself; if he remained where he was, a cursory inspection would reveal him. With no choice, he gripped the inside of the grille with his sweaty fingers, hoping he could keep his hold. The men were moving quickly through the room, and he exhaled as they passed him. Just as they were leaving the room, the phone vibrated. Ordinarily they never would have known, but he was on his stomach in the ventilation shaft and the phone was in his front pocket. The vibration echoed through the thin steel of the duct and they both turned.

They were eye to eye, the grille the only barrier between them.

"You've got nowhere to go," one of the men said with a Middle Eastern accent.

The other man did not have his partner's patience. He grabbed the grille with one hand and before Storm could release his hold almost pulled him out of the shaft.

"Okay," he said. "I'm coming out," he stalled, adjusting himself enough to remove the phone and stuck it down the front of his pants, hoping they would not search there. Half his body was out when the larger man grabbed him and yanked him the rest of the way. They frisked him, removing the screwdriver and knife from his pockets. Just before the man was about to search further, his radio went off. He pulled Storm to his feet and pushed him out of the room.

***

"They've got Storm." Alicia squirmed in her chair. Somehow Storm had been able to accept the call before being dragged out of the shaft, and though the sound was distorted, she could hear everything. She closed her eyes and tried to visualize his surroundings, as if she were the phone, and then realized she could be.

"Can you pull up the deck layout I sent Storm last night?" she asked Cody and started typing. She entered the phone number, found the carrier and within minutes had hacked into their server and had control of the phone. With a few keystrokes, she had activated the microphone and camera, then shot the image feed to one of the screens, but it was totally dark and she assumed it was in his pocket.

She heard the sound of footsteps on the steel deck, as well as his breathing, and guessed they were taking him someplace. Cody had the deck plan up on another screen, which she sent the GPS location feed to. Within seconds, from the comfort of the war room they watched the blue dot move through the passageways and stop in front of a door. Through the speakers, they heard the door creak open, and the dot moved into the room.

"Storm?" a voice asked.

"Mako?" Storm responded.

CHAPTER 18

Hillary had been making small talk and drinking coffee with the two guards when the alarm had sounded. Her cover had worked perfectly, but now she needed a way off the ship before they connected the dots. The alarm meant that Storm was in trouble, and he had given her specific instructions to get out if anything happened.

The moment the alarm had sounded, the guards had changed their demeanor. Succinct orders came through their radios in a language she couldn't understand, and they took off. The deck was empty, and she went for the stairs, listening for footsteps before taking the first flight two steps at a time. Then she slowed, thinking she looked guilty running. It took an effort, but she slowed her breath and started down the next flight, trying to remember how many levels she had climbed to reach the top deck. She could hear people yelling below and stopped by the swimming pool with two decks still below her. Easing herself into a small recess, she tried to think of what a real pilot would do if caught in the same situation—but she was a real pilot. Her training had taught her to evaluate the danger or threat and get out of harm's way, which was just what she was doing. Just act calmly and walk right off the ship.

She looked down at the pier and saw uniformed customs agents mixed in with a few local police yelling to one of the guards across the gangplank. The alarm suddenly turned off and the tension seemed to ease. She could hear the conversation below now, the guard telling the agent that it was just an equipment malfunction. Without the blaring klaxon, the scene was calmer. A police officer came to the agent's side and asked to speak to the captain.

The guard said something she couldn't hear, but she could tell from the reaction of the customs agent that it was not to his liking. She remembered some briefings on maritime law and knew how complicated the protocols were for boarding foreign ships. From the demeanor of the agent, she gathered that his request had been denied, and she watched him stomp off toward the building, but not before ordering the police officer to secure the boat—no one on or off. She was stuck.

For a brief second, she thought about trying to talk her way off, but changed her mind. She had left her passport and pilot's documentation on the sailboat, and even if she had them, there was always the chance that they would be confiscated—a risk she couldn't afford to take. She didn't even have a driver's license with her. Moving to the port side, facing the harbor, she looked down at the water below. The jump was doable, but the crystal-clear water would expose her—there was nowhere to hide. If anyone heard her, she would be caught, if not by the guards, then by the local authorities. Dealing with local law enforcement might be preferable to getting shot, but she decided against it. There were strict conduct rules for airline employees in foreign ports, and she knew if this was reported she could lose her job.

Now, caught between decks, she decided to go back to the helipad. At least she wouldn't look out of place there. She walked to the stairs and started up, only to be faced by a woman coming down. The metal stairway was too small to pass, and they stood there facing each other.

"Who are you?" the woman asked.

"Hillary Caitlen," she responded, thinking her real name might be useful if they checked her out.

"What are you doing here?" She asked.

"I was sent to pilot the helicopter," Hillary said, nervously knowing there was no verifying her story.

"You will come with me." The woman withdrew a small revolver from behind her back. "I was not aware of any flights this morning."

She led her into a passageway and pushed her through an open door that led to the bridge. Two uniformed men were there, running diagnostics on the equipment that Storm must have damaged.

"Did either of you know the helicopter was scheduled for anything this morning?" the woman asked the senior man.

He turned around, a distressed look on his face. "I've got my hands full here. Cyrus has ordered us to sea as soon as we ascertain the damage. You'll have to ask him."

"How bad is it?"

"Looks to be mostly computer systems. We're working on it," he said. "Thankfully we have manual controls for most it."

With her gun, the woman motioned Hillary to the door facing starboard and pushed her through the opening. She had remembered Storm mentioning the name Cyrus. If he was the owner of the yacht, she had to get off now; surely he would know this was a ruse. She looked over the rail at the pier below them—a hard fall from this height. It was quiet on the dock now, the only presence the officer guarding the gangway. She thought about yelling for help, but wasn't sure if he had the right to board, or would even take the chance himself. They had to know the diplomatic status of the owner by now.

Looking for a way out, she followed the woman's orders and descended to the deck below. At least they were getting closer to the water level in case she needed to escape. But her hopes faded as she was pushed through a pair of smoked glass doors with an insignia engraved in them. She entered the most luxurious living room she had ever seen—on land or sea. Despite her situation, she couldn't help but check out the lavish surroundings. Her eyes soon found two cold orbs staring back at her, and her blood froze.

They turned to look at the woman holding the gun. "We have another guest?"

"She says she was sent here to fly the helicopter." The woman pushed her toward a chair.

The man's eyes told her to sit.

"Mei Lan? Maybe she has something to do with this," he said, and turned to her. "Credentials?"

She breathed a sigh of relief at the reprieve.

One of the guards entered the room. "The customs agent is back with a warrant. It says he has the authority to search the ship before we leave," he said.

"Send the captain to stall them," he told the guard. "I am going to the bridge to check on the repairs." He got up and followed the guard.

The woman looked distracted, and Hillary wondered if this was her opportunity. She doubted her captor would risk gunfire with the customs agent and police officer on the pier. Looking back at the smoked glass entry doors, she thought about making a run for it, but the deck suddenly vibrated and the engines fired. It looked like her window for escape had disappeared.

***

Alicia was working furiously on several fronts: texting back and forth with Mako and Storm, searching for any radio traffic about the ship, and trying to locate Hillary.

"Cody," she called. He came in the room with a Coke and set it in the cup holder of the captain's chair. "Hillary—last name unknown. Flies the San Juan to Tortola route for Cape Air. I need you to find her cell number."

"Roger that," he responded, turning the chair to face the far screen and pulling up the keyboard.

Alicia turned back to what she had been doing. Cody would find the woman. She sat back, absorbing the satellite communications feed, letting her subconscious work on the numbers while her conscious mind debated with itself. She was unsure how to proceed. From the text messages sent by Mako, she knew exactly what the situation was and had evaluated the threat as dangerous but not critical. That meant she had a little time while the yacht was still disabled.

Cody was on the phone now, speaking into the microphone on his headset, using his friendliest Southern drawl to coax the information he needed from whoever he was talking to. Her eyes were suddenly drawn to the middle screen, a real-time satellite view of the harbor. A red icon had just flashed on the yacht. She reached for the phone and texted Mako. They had decided that it was critical to preserve what little battery life was left on the phone and had set out a communications schedule where he would turn the phone on every half hour. That was still almost twenty minutes away, but she texted anyway, asking what was going on. For the icon to appear, that meant that the ship's radar signal was operational and their power was likely back on. Whatever damage Storm had done to the generator had been at least temporarily repaired.

While she waited for Mako to respond, she went back to the CIA portal and opened a chat window. The senior agent in charge of the original contract was on the other end, and they were in the middle of a heated negotiation. The description of the two cases and the presence of Mei Lei and Mei Lan had rattled some cages at headquarters, and the agent was in on his day off. Alicia had explained her theory to the agent and was waiting for the Agency's analysis. The wheels were moving slowly, but with both China and Iran involved and more than a hundred pounds of weapons-grade uranium, along with the access to the codes to stop Nitro Zeus, this was probably going high up the ladder, and the higher it went, the longer things took. The screen of her phone flashed. Mako had just texted that the engines had started. The threat level in her head jumped a notch to critical.

"Got her," Cody said.

"Text her that we are trying to help and see if you can get any kind of status," she told him.

Alicia squirmed in her chair. She was stuck waiting, staring at the red icon on the screen, praying it didn't move and hoping for an alert to pop up from the Agency. Sitting here as an observer, unable to affect the outcome, was not a situation she was comfortable with.

***

* * *

The phone vibrated in Hillary's pocket, and she tried to hide her surprise from Mei Li, who was pacing the room behind her, talking in what she thought was Chinese to the younger woman she assumed was her daughter. The piano blocked their view of her, but she was hesitant to check the phone.

"Excuse me," she started and waited for them to turn. "Can I use the restroom?" She was surprised how easily the line came, then realized she really did need to go.

The older woman nodded toward a door to the side and continued her conversation. Hillary went for the door and entered a large room, nothing like she expected. She found herself in a spa. She couldn't help but look around at the sauna, steam room, and massage tables. Off to the side, she found another door that led to the actual bathroom, with a shower larger than her apartment.

She pulled the phone out and saw a text message from a Florida area code—someone not in her contacts—and was about to put the phone back in her pocket when she noticed the first few words of the text on screen said Mako. Sliding her finger across the notification, she opened the message app, which went automatically to the text.

Mako—can you help?

Yes, she typed back, *but being held on yacht.*

Info? was the response.

She typed quickly, not wanting to give the two women any reason to check on her. On her way back to the salon, she noticed the sauna and had an idea. Typing *diversion*, she went to the control panel for the sauna and hit the power button, hoping that was all she needed to do to start it. At the steam shower, she did the same thing, leaving both doors open. Not sure what it would actually accomplish, she exited the salon and made her way back to the chair.

The women were involved in a heated discussion now, but all three looked toward the glass door when it opened and Cyrus entered. He had their undivided attention when he spoke. "The repairs are almost completed, but the local customs agents want to board. That is unacceptable. We go now!"

***

"She says she will help, but is being held as well," Cody relayed the message. "Wait. She just texted again. Sounds like she is planning some kind of diversion."

"Shit," Alicia exclaimed and started typing, then pulled up another screen showing the Internet activity in the area. Fortunately it was early, in a late-night kind of spot, and the Internet was quiet. She found the Wi-Fi signal for the yacht. Getting into it would take some work, but would also allow her to monitor their status. With the damage that Storm had caused, she had no doubt that they would be working with tech support from the vendors of the equipment to facilitate repairs.

"Program's running. Knew that sucker would come in handy," Cody said.

"I'd give you a pat on the back, but I'm a little busy right now." They both stared at the numbers scrolling down the screen, showing every combination of letters, numbers and characters imaginable. Suddenly it stopped on *Shahansha1234.* They both looked at each other and laughed. She was into the ship's computer in seconds, amazed at the easy password, thinking it must have been set up by whoever had installed the router and never been changed. From her screen in Key Largo, she mirrored everything going on aboard the ship—when suddenly the communications stopped.

CHAPTER 19

Mako dropped the bottle opener when the engines fired. Fortunately only strands remained of his ties, and he pulled his arms apart, breaking the last of the fibers that had restrained him. The entire compartment echoed from the vibration of the machinery. He moved to Storm and quickly undid his ties. They were free now, except they couldn't communicate—the sound was deafening. Mako turned on the phone and activated the flashlight. It was so loud he could see Storm's lips moving, but no sound came out. He opened the note app screen, typed in: *Type it*, and held it in front of Storm's face.

Storm took the phone and ignored him. He used the light to check every wall, looking for a way out. There was nothing. The sealed hatch was the only access point. Without a cutting torch, they were stuck. Storm shut off the quickly dimming light and handed the phone back. The second Mako took it, the screen lit up, almost causing him to drop it.

Check the door, the message said. Mako turned the light back on and handed the phone to Storm. He read the text and held the phone so Mako could see the hatch. He moved toward it and cautiously turned the circular mechanism. It didn't move. He tried again, harder this time, and was about to give up and turn away when he felt something release in the latch mechanism.

They entered the passageway carefully, fully aware that the ship would be searched for the cause of the alarm. Mako paused before they climbed the stairs to the deck above and typed *Out* into the screen.

"We have to find Hillary," Storm yelled.

Outside of the sealed compartment, Mako could hear him now. "Where is she?"

"Text Alicia. If she has a phone, she can track the GPS," Storm said and pulled Mako with him into a recess.

They heard footsteps coming down the open metal treads of the stairway and pushed close to each other. Mako froze for a second, wondering if he had closed the hatch, but it was too late now. As soon as the men passed, Storm pushed him out of the alcove and they ran up the ladder to the deck above. They were in the crew's quarters now, still under the waterline, but this could be the safest place on the ship—if the guards did search their own deck, they would probably do so last.

Storm pulled him into a storeroom and closed the door. Mako typed in quickly: *Where is Hillary*?

They caught their breath while they waited for a response, surprised by the sudden quiet as the alarm was turned off. The ship vibrated and they felt it move.

"They're leaving. We have to get off," Mako said.

"Not without Hillary. Text her back and tell her it's urgent."

Mako typed in the message and waited. Alicia answered and they went back and forth in a quick conversation. Mako summarized for Storm. "She says Hillary's still onboard. The GPS signal is coming from her phone, but she lost access to the ship's controls when they left the pier and turned off the Wi-Fi."

"We have to see what's going on," Storm said and went for the door.

"But, she can tell us what to do. We should stay here," Mako said.

Storm turned to him. "Sooner or later you're going to have to man up, and now is a good time. Sometimes you have to see for yourself." He pushed out the door.

Mako followed him up the next flight of stairs and they found themselves on the main deck. They were on the port side, away from the dock, but even with the bulk of the ship between them and the dock, they heard men screaming orders to stop. Storm crept low and ran across the front of the salon. Mako followed behind him, glancing in the smoked glass doors. He did a double take when he saw Hillary held at gunpoint by Mei Lan. Storm was too far ahead for Mako to stop him, so he followed. They reached the starboard side and peered around the corner of an exposed section of bulkhead, shading the deck and holding a sun deck above.

Uniformed customs agents and police were screaming on the dock, their words hard to understand with their accents becoming thicker as they got more excited. The crew was ignoring them, untying the dock lines and dropping them overboard. With a jerk, the yacht, its bow thrusters disabled, tried to pull away from the pier, but without only the propeller, it was too slow to turn and slammed into the concrete piles. The captain powered forward again, hitting the other pile before finding enough water to turn. They almost fell to the deck as the ship accelerated.

The men on the pier were waving guns in the air, but not shooting, and they quickly became dots on the shore as the yacht hit cruising speed, ignoring the speed limit. The ship cut a wide turn, barely missing the boats in the mooring field, and finally found the marked channel and headed out toward blue water. Mako looked back at the shore and saw a large outboard loaded with men pull away from the dock and speed after them.

"Hillary's in the salon. Mei Lan has a gun on her," Mako told Storm.

"Shit. At least she's alive. I expect we have a little time while they sort this out." Mako followed his glance back to the speedboat behind them. A larger boat was now casting off its lines and moving out as well. "Twelve miles to international waters. I don't know if they'll catch us."

They were at least a half mile ahead, and it didn't look like the outboard was gaining. The larger boat that had started later was falling even further behind. The yacht made a turn to the west once they were clear of land, and the men looked at each other.

"Venezuela," Storm said.

Mako pulled the phone from his pocket, but Storm put his hand out. "I need to tell her," he said.

"She'll figure it out," Storm said. "What we need to do is get Hillary and get off this ship."

"You have a plan?" Mako asked.

"The helicopter, or that speedboat they have for a dinghy. Not sure about the chopper, but the boat's got a range of two hundred miles and can outrun the yacht."

"But how?" Mako asked.

"We need to wait this out until dark. Everything changes on a ship then," Storm said.

Mako did the math in his head, figuring they were doing forty knots. With sunset still eight hours away, they would be close to three hundred miles away by then. He pulled the phone out again and pulled up a map of the Caribbean. The app opened, showing a blue dot with their location. With the phone between them, they both made the same assumption. They would have to get off right after nightfall, before St. Croix was out of reach of the outboard or helicopter. Once they passed out of range, there was only open ocean and no cell service.

***

"You're a pretty girl," Mei Lan said, holding a knife to Hillary's face. "Tell me who you are and who you work for and I will spare your face."

Hillary struggled against the cord holding her hands together. "I told you. I am a pilot."

The knife brushed against her cheek, then slid down to her blouse. Mei Lan clipped the first button, and Hillary felt the cold steel against her breast.

"Maybe here instead," she said.

Hillary felt the pressure of the blade against her skin and cringed. She was just about to speak when the door burst open.

"They escaped," the crewman said.

"How?" Mei Lan hissed. She withdrew the blade and pointed it at the man.

Hillary noticed a drop of blood fall from the tip and realized it was hers.

She turned to Hillary. "I'll be back for you," she said and left with the man.

Hillary slumped in the chair, exhausted from the effort of just holding on. Her Navy training had covered capture, but not this situation. The woman was clearly unstable and sadistic. She tried her ties again, but they wouldn't yield. With the ship underway, she tried to sort through her options and realized just how limited they were. Just as she was about to give up hope, the door opened and she saw a familiar face.

"Hillary, are you okay?" Mako went for the ties on her wrists.

"Hold on," Storm said, stopping him. "We can't just break her out. We need a plan."

"You can't leave me here. Look what she did to me." She looked down at the spot of blood on her blouse.

"She's right," Mako said.

"Look, people. This is not going to work with all three of us running around holding hands. It's bad enough with the two of us. It's much better if she's here."

Hillary stared at him. "I can suck it up if you have a plan."

***

Alicia slammed her fists against the keyboard in frustration. There was nothing she could do. The ship had turned off the Wi-Fi, eliminating her access to its controls just after they left the dock. Fortunately they had not disabled the radar tracker, and she was able to watch the yacht's progress. The Agency had been notified and were supposedly calling the Navy in, but this was a tricky political situation. Taking an Iranian vessel in international waters to rescue Americans that were not supposed to be there did not fall under the guise of a standard operation.

Leave that to the Navy, she thought. She had gone into their computers through an old Agency link and seen that their closest assets were in Puerto Rico. There were no ships close enough to intercept the vessel if it maintained its current speed. The option of sinking it from the air was off the table with the suspected uranium aboard, never mind the three Americans.

She held off the temptation to text Mako and Hillary's phones in case they were or would be compromised. Cody came in, placed a mug of hot tea in front of her and rubbed her shoulders. She closed her eyes for the first time in hours and relaxed to his touch. But before she could fully succumb, she had an idea.

"What if it were one of your games?" she asked him.

"Hmm. Give me a minute." He went to the captain's chair. "Give me control of the map."

"Yes, sir."

"Populate it with known assets, please."

She watched him manipulate the screen as she placed the Navy ships and connected to the radar transponder showing *Shahansha*'s position. The cursor flew across the screen as he started plotting courses and intercept angles. Nothing worked.

"What does she have on board?" he asked.

"What do you mean?"

"Yachts that big have stuff. An outboard? Helicopter?"

She pulled up the last surveillance photo of the yacht at Costa Smeralda. "Helicopter—here, check it out. There must be an outboard, but from the deck plan, it launches from the lower level and is out of sight."

"Roll back the timeline. Didn't Mako say something about a speedboat chasing them the night before last?" Cody asked. They stared at the screen as time moved backwards, carefully watching the digital display showing hours and minutes on the top right of the screen. "There, stop it. Shit, is that an outboard?" Cody said and zoomed in on the boat. "Twin two seventy-fives is more than just an outboard. That sucker'll hit fifty knots if the conditions are right. But that's not their way out—this is." He zoomed in on the aft deck, where a helicopter was tied down to the deck. "Bell 429. I bet Hillary can fly it."

CHAPTER 20

"Wake up." Storm elbowed Mako.

He looked around, trying to get his bearings. The heat remaining in the sauna must have lulled him to sleep. "What time is it?"

Storm ignored the question. "I left you here to watch Hillary, and you fall asleep. Some things don't change," Storm said.

Mako pulled out the phone and turned it on. The screen remained dark, and he fiddled with the controls. "Is she okay?"

"I had a look around the ship. And yes, she's still there," Storm said.

"What about our course?" Mako asked, turning the dead phone in his hands.

"You don't get to play twenty questions," Storm said. "Now get your butt up, time to move out."

As soon as he gained his feet, he noticed the sway of the boat. "What's going on?"

"Wind kicked up," Storm said.

They crept out of the spa and into the salon, checking the room carefully before entering. The smoked windows concealed the true state of things outside. Mako went to the door, but pulled back suddenly. A guard passed. He continued on his rounds, and Mako exhaled.

"Can you be a little more careful?" Storm scolded him. He peered through the smoked glass and suddenly pulled the handle and opened it. They were met with a blast of air.

"Do you think you two can stop squabbling for ten seconds and get us out of here?" Hillary said. "It's like you're father and son."

The two men looked at each other, quickly turning away.

"That's it, then. I knew it—you are," she said. "Can't wait to see the childhood photo album. Bet there's all sorts of lovely memories there."

Both men ignored her. Storm stuck his head out the door and looked around the deck.

"Stay here with her. I'm going to check out the ship," Storm said and left the salon without looking back.

Mako went to the bar, surveyed its contents and poured four fingers of a thirty-year-old scotch. He brought it over to Hillary and held it to her lips.

"Might have preferred water, but this works too," she said.

"Any action while we were gone?" Mako asked.

"They brought me some food, and one of the guards checks in every so often, but that evil woman hasn't been back."

Mako's stomach rumbled at the mention of food. He went back to the bar, poured another drink and started searching the cabinets, removing a bag of nuts, which he took to the settee by her chair. Slouching down to be out of view of the door, they shared the nuts and scotch, made small talk and waited for Storm to return.

***

Storm crossed to the steps, climbing them two at a time. He stayed on the balls of his feet to avoid making any noise. The only access to the upper deck was a set of exterior stairs. Starting there, his plan was to work his way down. Voices came from an outside dining area on the next deck, and he waited, recalling the deck layouts. The ship was a labyrinth, and he needed a way around them. Following the plan, he crept around the corner, careful to stay out of sight. Peering around the bulkhead, he could see Cyrus and the two women. They were seated at a round table laden with food, but no one was eating.

He moved closer, trying to get within earshot, when something came up behind him. Without looking back, he hugged the wall and held his breath. The crewman passed by and went to the table, where he spoke to the group.

"You checked everywhere? I find that hard to believe," Cyrus said. "We know they are on the ship."

The man spoke again, clearly anxious about pleasing his master. "Everywhere. But there are only six of us. The woman is still there, but there is no sign of the two men. It is possible to play cat and mouse on a ship this large."

Mei Lan rose. "I will find them," she said.

"And how are you going to do what my men cannot?" Cyrus asked.

"Think like them. They know the longer the ship is out, the less of a chance they have to escape. It's either the helicopter or the speedboat. We don't need to search for them; they will come to us."

"Very thoughtful," Mei Li complimented her daughter. "Cyrus, listen to her."

He gave her the look only a father and daughter can exchange, and Storm wondered what Hillary had seen between him and Mako. He backed against the wall again as the man approached.

His problems had increased now that the only two means of escape would be guarded. Remaining where he was, he continued to listen to the conversation, confirming their destination as Venezuela. Once within helicopter range, they would be flown off the yacht to an airfield, where a private jet waited to take them to Iran. Storm knew he had to stop them, even if it meant disabling the helicopter and losing one of their means of escape.

After listening for a minute, he descended the stairs one flight at a time, carefully waiting and listening at each level. Finally he reached the lower deck, needing to somehow secure the speedboat for their escape. The deck was quiet, but he expected a guard to be placed by the launching area astern. Slowly he made his way through the passageway, listening for any unexplained sound until he reached a watertight hatch that opened to a large open deck. He pressed his body against the bulkhead, instinctively sucked in his stomach to narrow his profile to anyone outside, and moved to the open doorway.

The launch area looked like a garage, with a hydraulic transom that opened seaward like a garage door. Inside, the speedboat they had encountered earlier occupied one side, sitting on a sled-like device that would slide back, extending into the water to launch and retrieve the boat. The other side held two Zodiac inflatables lined up bow to stern. It was the speedboat that interested him. A guard sat against the speedboat with a rifle in his lap. Storm studied the controls for the door and lifts, knowing when they did go for it, they would have to be quick. Satisfied he could operate the machinery, he crept silently back through the ship to the salon.

***

* * *

"If I can get you to the helicopter, can you disable it?" Storm asked Hillary.

"Why break it if she can fly it?" Mako asked.

"Because if we fail, it delays them too," Storm said.

"Wait a minute." Mako held up his hands. "Wait a minute. She's the only one onboard that can fly it."

"I wouldn't assume that," Storm said.

"Would you two stop talking like I'm not sitting here?" Hillary said. "Enough of this. Cut me loose and let's get on with it."

Mako sat on the settee watching the two of them, his estranged father and this badass woman that he realized he liked more than he had been willing to admit. Things were moving away from his wheelhouse at an uncomfortable rate. His self-image was the cat burglar with James Bond charm, preferring to work alone and using his suave demeanor to avoid confrontation. This situation was leaning toward a violent conclusion. Cyrus had already bested him in London. He knew Mei Li's reputation, and her daughter was apparently cut from the same cloth.

There was something he could do. Something he knew he was better than Storm at, and that was finding the cases and the data. His confidence grew as he thought through a plan. He would need Alicia's help with the data, but this might still be salvageable.

"We need to split up," he said, waiting until they turned to face him before he continued. "I'll find the cases and secure the encryption code. You two take care of getting us out of here."

Storm looked at him with a tinge of pride in his cold eyes. "Very good."

They talked through the basic plan, knowing it would probably change, but they would have a starting point. Mako carefully checked the area outside before giving the all clear sign. Storm and

Hillary moved first, exiting in the direction of the exterior aft stairs. Mako watched as they descended, and when they were out of sight, he crossed the plush carpeting and descended the interior midship stairs to the main cabins. He was alone now, and his brain started to plant the seeds of doubt, exposing every pitfall of the plan. But with Alicia's help, he knew he could do this. Ducking into a closet, he pulled out his phone and looked at the dark screen —the battery was dead, he remembered. He was truly on his own now.

He drew a deep breath and started box breathing to calm his nerves. The technique taught at the Agency consisted of a four count in, hold for four, release, hold for another four and breathe in again. After repeating the cycle several times, he felt calmer and the pounding in his ears stopped. *Think like her*, he told himself. *If you were an encryption code, where would you be?* If something was that important, it would be in his cabin, he realized. Even though there seemed to be an amicable relationship between him and the Chinese women, that code was his.

He recalled the deck layouts and without the aid of his phone tried to plot a course to the cabin. It was one deck below as he remembered. He worked through another set of breaths and left the closet.

The decks were empty, and he made his way quickly down the stairs and through the passageway. Two open doors were across from each other, and a larger, more decorative door stood as a barrier at the end of the corridor. He glanced in each open room, figuring they were taken by the women, and continued to the closed door. He waited in front of it but realized that he was too exposed. Slowly he turned the handle and pushed the door open, surprised by the feel of the solid wood. The room appeared empty, and he entered, crouching low and using a sitting area adjacent to the door to screen himself. He waited there for a few minutes until he was confident he was alone. Standing, he surveyed the room and saw a laptop sitting on a desk. He approached it as if it was booby-trapped, and he realized how much he missed Alicia in his ear. As much as he hated her ordering him around, she was much better at this than he was.

He opened the cover, jumping when the machine spun to life and the screen lit up. He sat in front of it, staring at the icons and wondering what to do.

***

Storm led Hillary forward and down the midship stairs, entered the cabin on the main deck and found the service stairs to the crew and mechanical decks. His plan was to eliminate the guard at the boats and prepare a diversion. They would then find Mako and take the helicopter. If that failed, they would at least disable it and go back for the boat. Hillary was close behind him as they moved back to the open door leading to the boat garage. The man was still sitting where Storm had last seen him, and without a pause he entered as if he belonged there, taking the guard by surprise. Before the man could raise his gun or sound an alarm, Storm was on him, using an aluminum paddle he found in one of the smaller boats to choke him.

He had the element of surprise and pulled with all he had. The guard dropped the gun as he brought both hands to the paddle shaft to ease the pressure. The rifle slid toward the water, and before Hillary could grab it, it was swallowed by the sea. He turned his attention back to the guard, but the glance had cost him. The guard was powerful. Stronger than he was. With a grunt, the larger man stomped on his foot and elbowed Storm in the ribs, causing him to lose his grip and release the oar. They were toe to toe now, the larger man's face red from the surprise and the few seconds without air, but he had recovered from the surprise attack and charged Storm. Catching him with his shoulder to Storm's gut, he slammed his body against one of the smaller boats, causing it to slide on the skids supporting it.

"Get him in it!" Hillary screamed and charged.

Storm ducked under a punch and spun around, chopping the larger man in the back of his head with his elbow, but the man seemed unfazed and turned on him again. Desperately needing an advantage, Storm grabbed a fishing pole from a rack mounted on the wall. Swinging it like a fencing foil, he took the larger man by surprise, drawing blood with a quick parry to his face.

He moved forward in a classic fencing pose, pushing the guard further backwards with each parry and thrust. The action of the fiberglass pole was similar to a foil, and he effortlessly swung at the man. The deck heaved as the ship plowed through a wave, causing the Zodiac to shift again. He whipped the pole back and forth, trying to gain enough space to think, and risked a glance at Hillary. She was in the boat, priming the fuel line.

With a nod, he heard the engine start. It sputtered, unhappy there was no water, but she pushed in the choke and it settled down. "Now!" she yelled, popping the lever into reverse and turning the handle to full throttle.

Storm swung faster now, forcing the guard to back into the gunwale, and with a quick thrust pushed him into the boat. Hillary jumped forward and caught him with a chop to the temple. She jumped out, and he ran to the control panel. In one motion, the transom door opened like a ramp, and the sled that held the Zodiac slid back into the water. The engine caught and the outboard backed away from the ship, but with no one at the controls, it made a large circle and slammed into the lowered door. It spun around again, missing this time, and straightened out. They watched it for a few seconds and saw the man rise above the gunwales and try and take control of the craft, but it was too far behind the yacht, and the small engine didn't have the horsepower to catch the larger vessel.

"One down," Hillary said.

"Not out of the woods yet," Storm said and led her back through the door.

CHAPTER 21

Mako's heart jumped into his throat when he heard the door open. Fortunately the desk was in an alcove and not visible from the door. Carefully he closed the cover of the laptop and went for an open closet door. Just as he closed the door, he heard voices outside.

"I just got a message from one of my connections that the American's NSA office has issued an alert," a woman said.

He cracked the door. Mei Li and Cyrus stood only feet away.

"Our timeline has already been accelerated as much as I dare. The army will barely be ready to receive the material," Cyrus replied.

"Those cases need to get to your country before they can be identified as coming from China. That was the deal. We are dealing with you, not those crazed ayatollahs currently squandering your dreams of an empire," Mei Li said.

"We are en route to Venezuela, where I will disembark and fly directly to Iran. The material will be secure within twenty-four hours." He paused. "And what of the spies onboard? I thought you and your daughter had that under control." There was a heavy emphasis on "daughter."

"She's your daughter too. Maybe her instability comes from the

Persian blood."

"Enough of this. You insisted on raising her in China. She doesn't even know I am her father," he said.

"And that is for the best," Mei Li replied. "Unless, of course, this succeeds. Then she is in line for the succession, as we agreed."

Static from a radio interrupted them. Mei Li fumbled with the controls until the voice came in clearly, and Mako heard the distressed report. "We have trouble. One of the tenders was cut loose with a crewman in it."

"Go back for him," Cyrus said.

"No. We must keep our course," she replied. "I am going to see what is happening." She turned away to leave.

"Wait! My laptop is gone!"

Mako froze, the computer clutched under his arm. He hadn't meant to take it, just the data, but here it was.

"Are you sure it is not in the upper salon?" Mei Li asked.

Mako prayed for a miracle and got it. He heard them leave and cracked the door wider, carefully observing the stateroom before leaving the cover of the closet. He looked down at the desk, thinking for a moment about replacing the computer, but changed his mind. Cyrus already knew it was gone. Without Alicia's help, there was no time to parse the drive and find what he was looking for, even if he was capable of doing it. And he had no way of contacting her now.

With the computer under his arm, he stayed against the wall and slid toward the door. Peering into the empty passageway, he took a deep breath and ran to the stairs. The helipad was two levels above him, and he stopped suddenly at the landing. Footsteps echoed, and he waited to see which direction they were coming from. He heard a grunt below him and ran up to the next deck, where he looked out at the swimming pool and saw several figures huddled against the rail. They must be watching the tender. He took advantage of the distraction and ran toward the stern and up the final flight of stairs to the top deck.

The top deck was empty, and he ran for the helicopter, where he stashed the laptop under a mat in the cargo compartment. Now he had to find Hillary and Storm.

***

"What are you doing?" Hillary asked Storm.

He had made a sudden stop on the way from the boat launch and entered the engine room. Tools were scattered across the floor, but the room was empty. Apparently the search for them was more important than repairing the damage he had done earlier. It hadn't had the effect that they had hoped for anyway, but this time, now that they knew he was onboard, there was no need for stealth. Grabbing a pair of channel lock pliers, the biggest tool present, he started pulling and hacking at the exposed wires.

"Find those blasted alarms," he yelled to Hillary.

He continued the destruction, stopping only for a second as the first alarm sounded.

"Here!" she called from across the room.

He went to her and with the jaws of the pliers pulled several circuit boards from their homes. The alarms stopped. Suddenly the deck lurched under his feet, and he knew he had achieved success. The boat was out of control, yawing in the seas.

Still holding the wrench, he looked behind to make sure she was following before leaving the room with her in tow. He ran down the passageway toward the stairs. By his count there were five more crewmen, including the captain, and Mei Li, Mei Lan and Cyrus aboard. He gripped the wrench and climbed the first flight of stairs, expecting to meet resistance any second.

Just as they made the first landing, he ran head-on into a uniformed man. From the bars on his epaulets, Storm assumed it was the captain and he stopped. The man had a panicked look on his face, clearly not wanting a confrontation—just wanting to save his ship. But Storm didn't want the ship to be saved. He cocked his arm and with as much of a controlled effort as he was capable smashed the wrench into the man's forehead.

They left the body where it was, the need for stealth totally gone now. He started up the next flight of stairs but lost his balance as the ship was flung sideways by a large wave. Without her thrusters and rudder, she was at the whim of the seas, which would easily turn her beam to the waves, making capsize a real possibility.

Storm knew it was only a matter of time before the inevitable happened. They were on the third level now, with two more to go. He stopped and waited for his breathing to slow, listening for any pursuit. Footsteps came from above, more than one man by the sound of them. A quick look around showed nowhere to hide. Storm pushed Hillary into the passageway and ducked down the lower flight, trying to surprise them. He could hear the footsteps right above now and he crouched down, waiting.

Suddenly the first man was around the corner and facing him. Storm ambushed the man, swinging the wrench wildly and catching him full in the head. Blood shot from the wound, and he instinctively ducked to avoid it, but the other man was still coming and he needed a more substantial weapon. He rolled the downed crewman on his back and found the gun holstered at his side. Removing it and an extra clip, he slid the mechanism and chambered a round.

The next man saw him, and it looked like an old-fashioned shootout with both men drawing weapons at the same time. But just as he was about to shoot, Storm saw a leg sweep out of the passageway and the man came flying toward him. "Thanks for that," he said. He checked him for weapons, removing another gun from the downed man and pulled a handful of cable ties from his pocket.

"Bind them," he said, tossing them to Hillary.

Hillary caught them and went to the men, fighting to place the narrow plastic into the slot when another large wave threw her off balance. Finally, she nodded to Storm that the job was done.

The body count was now four, but the most dangerous were still at large. Down to two crewmen, the women and Cyrus, Storm started up to the next deck, but before he could reach the landing, shots fired, ricocheting off the steel stairs. He grabbed Hillary and they huddled together in the passageway while he evaluated the threat.

There was at least one man coming down the stairs. He leaned into the stairwell and fired two shots before ducking back. "The exposed bulkhead on the port side by the sun deck," he told Hillary. "Climb it." The decorative openings the architects had placed could be used as a ladder. "Go for it, I'll cover you. Find Mako and get the chopper ready." He fired another shot to hold off the pursuer, glancing back to check her progress. She reached the structure, and he waited until she had started up, easily grasping the openings, before firing another shot and running down the stairs. Now that she was close to the helicopter, he needed to find the cases.

Reaching the next level, he waited, trying to determine where they would stash the valuable cargo. There was no way the cases would be in a storage hold. If he knew Mei Li, they were close. A deck plan was posted by the exit from the stairwell, and he went to it, fighting off the wave of nausea brought on by the heaving ship as he tried to read the small plan. He located the staterooms on the next deck and ran down the stairs, using his momentum to pull himself around the corner before his pursuer saw him. Hopefully he would think Storm was heading for the speedboat and continue down.

He found himself in a garishly decorated passageway with doors on opposite sides and a larger ornate one at the end. Assuming that to be Cyrus's, he went to the port-side cabin and with the gun extended opened the door. The room was empty, and he quickly searched the cabin. He knew right away it was one of the women's, and from the style of clothes figured it to be Mei Lan's. After a cursory look, he ran across the corridor to the other room.

The door was ajar. It was too late when he realized it had been closed when he first looked. He pushed it open only to find a gun pointed at his head.

"Well, John Storm, we meet again," Mei Li said.

***

Mako froze when he heard the gunshots below him. He listened and peered around the glass-enclosed cockpit for any sign of pursuit. Seeing none, he left the cover of the helicopter and ran across the exposed deck to the stairs leading to the lower decks. Before he hit the first tread, he pulled himself back. More shots fired, and he retreated back toward the helicopter. The top deck had little for cover, only an open-air bar with a cantilevered roof above, and several deck chairs. Just that and the helicopter. He almost fell when the boat yawed on the crest of a large wave, the motion accentuated this high above the seas. Chancing a look over the side, he knew the ship was rudderless, her length parallel to the large wind-driven swells. The wind whipped his hair around, and he turned to the helicopter. This was their best chance to get out of this mess, but if he was caught up here, there was a chance it could be damaged and the laptop found. He needed to find Storm and Hillary.

Not wanting to risk the stairs, he leaned over the edge of the deck and saw Hillary climbing toward him. He held up a hand and motioned that he was coming down. She stopped and started descending the fiberglass wall. When she was close to the deck, he started after her. Together they huddled against the exposed bulkhead.

"Where's Storm?" Mako asked.

"Went to draw them off and find the cases," she said, trying to catch her breath.

They stood looking at each other, and he felt an awkward sensation with her eyes focused on him, something he had never felt before. Not wanting to deal with his feelings right now, he looked away, trying to figure out what to do. From somewhere within him came the desire to keep her safe.

"I'll find him. You go on up and get the helicopter ready," he said and instinctively reached for her. He hadn't meant to do it, but she fell into his arms and their mouths met.

A gunshot startled them, and they broke the embrace, both realizing that they had gotten lost in the moment. Another shot fired and Mako urged her up. Once she started climbing, he turned to the stern, the direction he thought the shots had come from. The decks tapered back with each level, and he could clearly see the edge of the boat launch.

CHAPTER 22

It was a standoff, Mei Li and Storm standing only feet apart with guns pointing at each other, both knowing the other wouldn't hesitate to shoot. Storm felt the emotion of their history flood through him, and from the look in her eyes he suspected she was going through the same thing.

"Where is it?" Storm demanded. "Even you know this is crazy. Iran with a nuke is no good for anyone."

"It will no longer be Iran. Once Cyrus has the power, it will be Persia again—in all its greatness," Mei Li said.

"King of Kings—yeah, I know my history," Storm said, scanning the cabin for the cases.

"They are not here. Do you think we would be so foolish to leave them on the ship?"

Storm stared at her, trying not to let the frustration show on his face. The trip to Jost Van Dyke had been a ruse, designed to draw them away from the uranium. He could only hope that Mako's capture and his work to disable the ship had accelerated their timeline. The cases might still be in the area, and if he played this right, they would lead him to the cache. He was so focused on his rival that he had forgotten his tradecraft for a second, and it had cost him. Instead of sidestepping away from the doorway when he entered, he had left his back exposed. The cold steel of the barrel pressed against the back of his head.

"Drop it," Cyrus said.

Storm hesitated, but knew he had no choice. The only way to find the uranium was to stay alive. As much as he would have liked to take Mei Li into the fires of Hell with him, he dropped the gun.

"Go ahead," Mei Li said. "There's no reason to keep him alive."

"And ruin the carpet? Tie him up. I have an idea to use him to lure out the other one," Cyrus said.

Mei Li lowered her weapon, giving Cyrus a clear shot at him. He tried to remember everything he could about the Iranian, calculating whether he would really pull the trigger. There was no doubt Mei Li would have shot him, but his gut told him Cyrus wouldn't. But he had been wrong before. The decision was made for him when the yacht rolled again, throwing all three off balance.

Storm felt the wave and anticipated the reaction. He braced himself for the initial thrust, knowing in just seconds the ship would roll back the other way as it settled into the next trough. He felt the yacht pause, and just before it slid back, he grabbed the gun on the floor and went for Mei Li. He stayed low, attacking hard and fast, before she could regain her balance. Her leg buckled backwards as she fell, and he felt a bone snap as she screamed in pain. Seizing the moment, he grabbed her by the hair and yanked her head back.

He had to restrain himself from shooting her right then for all the trouble she had caused him over the years, but he restrained himself. "Where are the cases?" He stared at Cyrus.

The dull orbs didn't respond. "Go ahead and satisfy your bloodlust. I no longer need her." He turned and ran from the room.

The ship yawed again, but this time Storm was taken by surprise, and he felt the sharp bone of Mei Li's elbow slam into his rib cage. Stunned for a second, he released her. She went for the door, but stumbled, screaming in pain. Hopping on one leg, using the wall of the corridor for support, she tried to follow Cyrus, but Storm regained his footing. Cyrus was right—she was of no use to either of them—and in a fit of rage, he aimed and fired. She fell to the deck, blood spraying from the wound. It was ironic, he thought, that the crimson blood was invisible, swallowed by the garish carpeting and wallpaper. Slowly he rose to his feet and looked down at her, feeling a strange kind of remorse for killing her. She had become so familiar to him over the years that her death took a part of him with her.

Shaking off the feeling, he rose and went after Cyrus. The passageway was empty, but he suspected he knew where the man was going. Stepping over a body, he entered the stairwell. There was no need for caution with the crew dispatched, and he flew down the stairs. At the bottom of the second flight, he saw Cyrus round the corner and enter the hatch leading to the boat garage. He aimed to take the speedboat and escape.

Storm had a clear shot as Cyrus ran ahead of him, but he stopped short of pulling the trigger. He needed him alive if he was to find the uranium. The encryption code was important, but without the threat from the weapons-grade material, it was useless. Let Mako *deal with that*, he thought.

A shot fired, causing him to flinch as he entered the hatch leading to the launch area. He needed Cyrus alive if he was to recover the material, but the opposite was not true. Cyrus fired again, and he felt something hot burn his shoulder. Blood trickled out of the wound, but he forced himself to ignore it. Cyrus climbed aboard the speedboat and started the engines. The transom was already lowered, and the tie downs were released from the boat. Storm fired, but a wave threw him off balance and the rounds went wild.

The shots caused Cyrus to pause, giving Storm enough time to grab the bow rail. His shoulder burned, and his feet dragged through the water as the hydraulic lift dropped the boat into the water. Cyrus jammed the engines into reverse. They whined as he accelerated, and the propellers grabbed water, pulling the boat out of his grasp.

There was nothing Storm could do to stop him; he could only watch him grin as he spun the wheel, turning the boat back toward land. Storm braced himself and aimed for the engines. Another wave hit just as he shot, disrupting his aim, but he recovered, and with his belly on the steel deck, he extended the gun with both hands in front of himself. He evened his breath and waited for the yacht to reach the crest of the next wave. Slowly, the stern raised as the bow fell into the trough, and he aimed down at the engine cowlings.

Facedown on the deck, Storm watched as Cyrus turned and pushed the throttles forward. He had only seconds before the boat would be out of range, and he took advantage of the prone position he found himself in. Placing both hands on the gun, he aimed and fired two quick rounds at the engines. Without waiting to see if one had hit, he jumped into the inflatable Zodiac and released the bow hook. With its twin already gone, the boat slid into the water and he fired the engine. Slamming the throttle forward, he spun the wheel, nearly missing the yacht, and sped after Cyrus.

***

* * *

Mako watched the speedboat pull out with Cyrus at the helm. He wondered where Storm was, but knew his first priority was the escaping boat. He turned around and went for the stairs, reaching the top deck at the same time as Hillary. Together they ran toward the helicopter. This high off the water, the wind was whipping, adding to the effect of the seas pushing them sideways across the deck. They fought against the gusts to reach the helicopter, and Hillary yelled at Mako to remove the tie downs.

She entered the left-hand door, and he could hear the engine start as he released the last restraint holding the Bell to the deck. The wind had picked up and the waves were growing and coming closer together. Mako barely dodged the skid when the helicopter slid sideways. He could hear the engines wind and the RPMs increase. Grabbing for the door, he yanked it open and pulled himself in.

"Hold on, this is going to be dicey," Hillary yelled over the engines and placed the headset on her head.

Mako grabbed his headset, remembering the first time he had talked to her over one. He yanked on the harness and buckled himself in, grabbing the side rails on his seat as the chopper tried to lift from the deck. The propeller grabbed for air, but another wave had the ship, and the deck pitched the wrong way, grounding them momentarily.

Hillary realized her mistake and waited for the deck to pitch the other way before pulling back on the stick. They were airborne now, and she quickly increased speed to gain altitude and avoid the yacht. Mako's stomach lurched as she tilted the control left and the chopper swung away from the superstructure.

They were clear of the yacht now, with no obstructions to block the scene unfolding ahead. There were two boats now, and Mako clenched his fists, rooting unconsciously for Storm, who he saw at the wheel of the smaller boat. Several sets of waves separated them, their crests high enough that until Hillary gained altitude, one of the boats was always hidden by a wall of water. They flew higher and turned, following the two boats.

The boats were no match for the helicopter, and they were quickly hovering above them. Smoke spewed from one of the twin outboards, and Mako watched as the Zodiac flew over the waves, gaining on the speedboat. Hillary was descending now, and Mako tried to think of some way to help Storm when he felt something behind him.

"This is convenient."

They both looked at each other and glanced back at Mei Lan pointing a gun at them from the jump seat.

"Shit," Hillary said and jerked back on the control. The G force pinned them to their seats as the nose of the Bell pulled up, but she still held the gun.

"Very good. Now we'll leave those two boys to take care of themselves. Next stop is Virgin Gorda."

Mako chanced another look back at her and saw the computer on her lap. She held all the cards now.

***

Alicia sat on the edge of her seat. She was confused by the signals with only the radar transponders available to her. She was able to determine that the *Shahansha* was disabled and had communicated that to the Navy. But now, without a visual, she was confused.

"Chopper is hovering over the speedboat, moving away from the yacht."

She was about to ask how he knew this, but as a gamer, the random action of the dots would seem logical to him. He might see it, but she stared at the screen, the dots meaning nothing to her. "Cody, can you go back through the footage and get the tail number on the chopper?" She watched him spin in his chair.

He took over the right-hand screen, zooming in on different angles of the satellite footage. She turned back to her station and opened another of her secret weapons. After she entered the coordinates where the chase was unfolding, the program found several VHF repeaters, giving her access to the local frequencies. She patched herself in to channel sixteen and hailed any vessel in the area—but none responded.

"What are they doing going back to Virgin Gorda?" Alicia asked out loud and relayed the information to the Agency.

CHAPTER 23

Under ordinary circumstances, the speedboat would have been easily able to lose the smaller and less powerful Zodiac, but with the heavy seas and disabled engine, the two craft were well matched. Storm watched the spray fly from the deep V of the speedboat as it plowed through the waves, fighting a losing battle to get on plane without the horsepower provided by the second engine. The Zodiac, on the other hand, was made for these conditions.

Storm, though not a novice, had little experience with an inflatable in these seas. He had a death grip on the wheel and was learning to ride the swells as he followed the trail of smoke from the speedboat's blown engine. Satisfied that the other boat was traveling at the same speed, he thought about his options. Ideally, he would capture Cyrus, deliver him to the Agency and let them work their special blend of magic on him, but right now, he was more concerned about stopping him.

In the distance, he saw what he thought were the hills of St. Croix on his port side, but knew Cyrus would never stop on American soil. The Zodiac lacked in electronics, and he had no choice but to follow the smoke. His shoulder throbbed, but the bleeding had subsided, and he bit his lip as another wave grabbed the inflatable and thrust it forward. Everything he tried in order to control the boat proved futile. All he could do was follow. The windblown waves were crashing over the bow, soaking him and obscuring his vision, but he squinted and kept his focus. There was nothing technology or Alicia could do for him now. Flying across the tops of ten-foot waves, he was on his own.

The smoke seemed to make a course change to the northeast, and he tried to remember the layout of the islands. He knew the British Virgins lay ahead, but his dead reckoning skills couldn't tell him where in the islands Cyrus was headed. Fuel was another concern, and he looked at the needle of the gas gauge, bouncing wildly with each bump the small craft took. He tried to average the fluctuations and decided he had three-quarters of a tank left. The only problem with that knowledge was that he had no idea how much fuel the tank held or the efficiency of the engine.

Storm's eyes stung from the spray, his hands were numb from their death grip on the wheel, and his shoulder burned as if a hot poker had been shoved into his flesh; finally, he decided enough was enough. It was time to make his move. Removing one hand from the wheel, he tentatively pushed down the throttle. The boat jumped forward, launching him over the wheel as it crested the wave too quickly. Frustrated, he recovered and pulled back on the throttle. With the seas this size, he was limited in maneuverability. With years of experience, he applied what he knew held true on land to the water. Keep Cyrus in sight, and an opportunity will present itself. He knew this wasn't the worst option and settled in for the ride. As long as the smoke trail remained, he was no worse off.

The roar of an engine took him by surprise and he looked up, seeing a helicopter moving fast overhead. His vision was streaked from the salt spray, but he was sure it was the Bell from the yacht.

***

Mako sat in the right-hand seat, powerless to do anything. With Mei Lan holding a gun and the computer, he was just along for the ride. Hopefully an opportunity would present itself when they landed, though he had no idea of their destination. She was shifting around behind him. Through the corner of his eye he could see her open the computer, but the gun remained pointed at them.

On the horizon he thought he saw a thin trail of smoke seemingly on the same course as the helicopter, and he stared down at the roiling sea, wondering how much trouble Storm was in.

"Fly toward the smoke," Mei Lan's voice came through the headset. "Not too low."

Hillary adjusted the controls, and the chopper dropped and turned towards the black streak. They closed quickly, moving much faster than the boats restrained by the water conditions. Another boat, smaller than the smoking speedboat, appeared behind it, and he thought he saw Storm at the helm. A funny feeling came over him as he realized he was rooting for his father, maybe for the first time he could remember. The boats were about a hundred yards apart, keeping pace with each other.

"Lower and close on the inflatable," Mei Lan ordered.

With the gun pointed at her head, Hillary had no choice but to obey, and the chopper dropped again. She reduced speed and they could clearly see Storm in the Zodiac. The pressure in the cabin dropped, and the Bell jerked when Mei Lan opened the door and fired at the boat below. Mako risked a glance at Hillary, who jerked the controls a bit more, throwing off the accuracy of the shooter.

"The next one's for you if you don't fly this level," Mei Lan said.

"It's the wind…" Hillary started.

Mei Lan shifted the gun to Mako. "Maybe this will clear your head. You fly right or lover boy gets it."

Hillary leveled off the chopper and they stared at the small craft below. If Storm had seen them, he was not acknowledging, and Mako noticed the red blotch on his shoulder.

Mei Lan must have seen it too. "Take us up to the other boat," she ordered.

Hillary pushed the stick forward, and Mako breathed a sigh of relief that Storm was out of immediate danger. The smoke trail thickened as they closed on the speedboat, and Hillary veered to port. She pulled even and matched the boat's speed. All three of them stared down at Cyrus.

Mei Lan yanked open the door and yelled down to the boat, screaming at Hillary to drop altitude. Mako wondered for a minute if she was crazy enough to attempt a rescue in these conditions and then saw the opposite was true. Gunshots fired, and the other engine soon flared and died. The boat slowed and stopped. In seconds it was turned abeam to the seas—powerless.

"Full power to the tip of Virgin Gorda. I will give you the destination as we approach," she ordered.

Mako wondered what this was all about. She had clearly meant to harm him or leave him stranded in the ten-foot seas. And then he remembered having heard the one word that might account for her actions—succession. She knew her destiny and had chosen not to wait. He looked back again and saw the Zodiac close on the helpless speedboat, but they were moving quickly and the small boats were soon out of sight. Focusing his attention forward, and with his eye for the female figure, he noticed the outline of the "fat virgin" ahead and wondered if this was the line of sight Columbus had first seen her from when he made landfall here five hundred years ago.

The island was approaching quickly, and Mako could see the straight line of a landing strip graded parallel to the ocean. He assumed they would be landing there, but just as they crossed land, Mei Lan's voice came over the headset.

"The abandoned copper mine." She pointed to a grouping of stone ruins set on an outcropping a hundred yards back from the ocean.

The helicopter made landfall and cruised by the ruins. Hillary circled, scanning the area. "There's nowhere safe to land there," Hillary said.

"There." She pointed to a barren area covered with rocks.

"It's sketchy," Hillary said. "It might look smooth, but if one of the skids hits a rock, we could roll."

"Never mind that. Land," Mei Lan ordered and pushed the barrel of the gun to Mako's head. "Now."

Hillary circled back and hovered over the semi-cleared area. Dropping speed, she guided the Bell toward land. The first skid touched and the chopper rocked on the unstable footing. She fought to control the craft, and finally the other skid settled.

***

Storm breathed a sigh of relief as the helicopter moved away. He looked around for damage, but the shots had all missed, and he wondered if whoever had shot at him thought the red splotch on his shoulder was their work. The chopper was hovering over the speedboat now, and he looked on in surprise as the other engine started smoking.

The boat had lost power and was abeam to the seas. He approached cautiously, not knowing if Cyrus had a weapon. He slowed to approach from the side, not wanting the waves to affect him. The Zodiac reacted favorably to the changes and settled in the trough. Without the need to control the boat through the waves, he released his right hand and reached behind him for the gun. Without the roar of the engines and within sight of Virgin Gorda, he tried to figure some way to communicate the situation to Alicia.

He saw the VHF, but before he could pick up the microphone, the two boats touched and he focused on the speedboat. Cyrus stood at the helm, trying frantically to restart the engines. Storm braced himself with the gun extended in his hand, thinking he might get a clear shot off, but the seas tossed the small boat, making aim impossible. A wave broke his concentration, and the Zodiac was tossed against the hull of the speedboat. The brief seconds he had taken to try and shoot his adversary had cost him.

The bow of the Zodiac was jammed between the starboard engine and the transom of the speedboat, held in place by the force of the seas. He fought the wheel, trying to untangle the two boats. The Zodiac rocked with the speedboat, the horsepower from its single engine insufficient to move it away from the larger boat. He pulled the throttle back, instinctively looking behind him, and felt the trim of the small craft change.

Turning back, he saw Cyrus jump from the transom and land on the bow of the Zodiac. He picked up the gun and fired, but the force of the impact and the Iranian's weight had separated the boats, and the shot went wild as the Zodiac swerved backwards.

Cyrus took the opportunity and lunged for him. Just as he was about to strike, they were rocked by the concussion from an explosion. The speedboat was in flames and both men spun to watch the fireball as it pushed high into the sky. Storm turned back first and grabbed Cyrus in a sleeper hold, squeezing his neck to cut the blood flow from the carotid artery to disable the man. Cyrus fought back, striking several blows to Storm's head, but the deck space on the outboard was limited, and he couldn't get any force behind the punches.

The two men were tangled together now, their weight pinning them against the gunwale of the Zodiac, when a wave came over the stern. Water flooded the cockpit, soaking them. Storm risked a quick look behind. Still in reverse, the counterclockwise spin of the propeller was pulling the boat in an ever-tightening circle. They were abeam to the seas now, and he waited until the boat spun into another ninety degrees before making his move.

The stern was on the face of the wave, the forward momentum surfing the boat backwards. Just as the wave crested, the Zodiac was hurled forward, its speed increasing with the force of the wave. He used the change to push Cyrus off and slam his head into the stainless steel bracing supporting the T-top.

Cyrus appeared to be unconscious, and Storm went for the gun, but without anyone at the helm, the seas grabbed the boat and spun it. Another wave crashed over the transom, flooding them again. Water was halfway up the gunwales now, the weight slowing the boat. Forgetting about Cyrus for the moment, he went back to the helm and pushed the throttle forward. It took a few seconds, but he wrestled control back from the waves and straightened the boat out.

Cyrus was still unmoving on the deck, but there was nothing he could do to restrain him. All his efforts needed to go into saving the boat from sinking. Stuck at the helm, he had to do something about the water in the cockpit. Taking his eyes off Cyrus, he gunned the boat until the self-bailers had drained all but the last few inches of water.

With Cyrus unconscious on the deck, he looked around at the barren seas, the only sign of land the tip of a peak several miles in the distance. Remembering the VHF, he called for any craft in the area and was surprised to hear Alicia's voice. She had him switch to channel seventy-two.

She answered directly and he explained the situation. The radio went silent for a few minutes.

"Come on. I need a destination," he said.

"The helicopter just landed at the abandoned copper mine on Virgin Gorda," she said and paused. "Mei Lan is on it."

"Well, that explains why they shot at me," he said and changed course. The seaward tip of the island lay directly ahead.

"There's an airstrip half a mile from the mine. It has to be connected."

CHAPTER 24

Alicia stared at the static image of the copper mine on the screen, frustrated that she could do nothing but sit and watch. "There's got to be something we can do," she said, wishing she had access to the satellite controls that would give them an up-to-the-minute visual.

"Got an idea," Cody said.

She watched him pull up a drone forum and wondered what he was up to.

"Check it out. Two guys within a few miles," he said after scrolling through the membership. "This is gonna be awesome. Just wish I could run them remote."

"What are you talking about?" she asked.

"We get one of these guys to send a drone overhead. We'll have full visuals and maybe weapons capability."

"Weapons?"

"Still experimental. The retail models are too light to take up anything serious, but some of the commercial models are beefed up enough. Let's see what we have here."

"Nothing to lose, go for it," she said and turned back to her keyboard, but there was nothing to be done. Sitting back, she closed her eyes, trying to think of anything she could do to help them from a thousand miles away.

***

Once Storm changed course, the Zodiac was able to ride the swells toward Virgin Gorda instead of plow into them, and he was finally able to relax his grip. He looked around the deck for something to restrain Cyrus, who was still unconscious on the deck, but with the tip of the island less than a half mile away, he didn't want to risk leaving the wheel. As he approached, he looked for a place to beach the boat. As he closed, details of the shoreline came into view. Rocky cliffs rose from the water, offering no access. Finally he saw a cut around the ocean side and changed course. Cut into the rocky shore, what he guessed was a man-made channel by its straight lines and shape revealed itself. It wasn't much, just large enough to dock a ship. It would easily accommodate the small inflatable, and he steered toward it. The ruins were in sight now, and he could see the helicopter sitting off to the side by the crumbling remains of a stone tower.

Navigating into the cut was harder than he thought. Large swells gathered at each side of the entry, the conflicting pattern of the wind and seas bombarding the semi-protected cove from both sides. Waiting for a lull, the Zodiac yawed in the surf and picked up speed as Storm fought the controls. The seas overpowered the small boat and he thought they were going to crash into a large rock. Just before impact, a large wave picked up the small craft and heaved it onto one of the boulders. The water started to recede, and Storm knew this was his chance. He had to get out before the undercurrent from the wave took the boat back out to sea.

He jumped from the bow, landing on the boulder, but before he could gain his footing, another wave came and slammed him against the rocks. He tried to push himself up, but his shoulder crumpled under him. Seawater had permeated the wound, and he fought through the intense pain, rising onto one knee and crawling across the rocks to safety.

When he looked back, he saw the Zodiac still trapped in the cut, moving back and forth, a victim of the continuous battle between the waves and the undertow. Just as he was about to turn away, he saw Cyrus's head rise above the gunwale. Hoping the water hadn't damaged the gun in his belt, he turned and fired several rounds at the boat, but the wave action made it impossible to aim. For now, his first priority was the chopper, and he started to climb up the left bank toward a narrow chute extending up the hill.

He ran up the smooth surface of the chute, thinking it was probably a sluice box for the mine, although it looked newer. The footing was good and he reached the top of the hill. Once there, he dropped to his knees and ducked behind a low block wall for cover. On his right were the remains of the mine, the rough-hewn stone construction a stark contrast to the newer precast block structure surrounding him, but this was no time to be an archeologist.

The chopper was off to his left in a small clearing, but a quick glance revealed no one there. He broadened his surveillance, scanning the hilltop, looking for Mako and Hillary, but there was no sign of them. Needing a better vantage point, he ran to the remains of the old building and entered the decrepit structure. Crossing to the far wall, he hid behind the corner stones, the only remaining part of the wall, and saw three figures staring down into what looked like a cistern surrounded by a low stone wall.

A pink cab caught his eye, and he followed its path as the driver wound up the steep road to the parking lot. The mine was a state park, but off the beaten path so it got few tourists compared to the more popular beaches. The sight of the cab with only the driver looked out of place. Turning back to the cistern, he saw Mei Lan, with a gun in one hand, lift a welded wire grid covering the opening and push Hillary in. He could only watch as Mako turned to fight her. She lashed at him with the butt of the gun and caught his temple. Storm cringed as he watched him fall into the void and the lid drop back down. Two shots were fired, and he leaned back, expecting the worst.

The few seconds of mourning cost him. Suddenly he felt the toll the last few days had taken and was about to rise when something struck him in the head and he crumpled to his knees. Blood streamed across his face as he looked up at Cyrus standing over him, holding a rusty old piece of steel pipe. He was about to rise when he thought he heard a woman's voice call to him. Before he could react, Storm felt another blow from the cold steel knock him backwards.

***

"Is this cool or what?" Cody asked from the captain's chair.

Alicia had to admit it was, but he needed to realize that this was a life-or-death situation, not a video game. She watched the footage streaming from the drone to the screen in real time. Cody had contacted one of the two members of the forum, who happened to be a cab driver. He was free, and he loaded his drone and headed for the mine.

"Can you talk to him so I can get an overview?" Alicia asked.

Cody spoke into his headset. "Got it, putting it on speaker."

"Al, dude, you're on the speaker with Alicia and me. She needs to give you some direction."

"Cool, man, go ahead," he said. "But it's crazy windy. I can make her dance under better conditions, but this is going to be tricky."

Alicia stared at the screen and told him what she wanted. The drone ascended and started to circle the site. She understood now what he meant about the wind's effect on the machine, but although there was some movement, the picture was surprisingly good. The drone was over the Zodiac, still being tossed like a child's toy in the cove, but there didn't appear to be anyone there. The drone moved over to the ruins now, and she could see Mei Lan standing above a rectangular hole covered with wire.

"Can you go lower and see what they're looking at?" she asked Al.

"On the way," he responded.

The drone sped toward the area, and she saw the surprised look on Mei Lan face as she saw the craft hovering over her. If only it was weaponized, Alicia thought, she could take her out right now. But the opposite was true, and she flinched as Mei Lan aimed the gun and fired at the drone. The shot missed and the craft quickly gained altitude, but the woman pursued and fired again.

"Cody, can you enhance the footage?" she asked.

He pulled the feed to another screen and reversed the video. Alicia was disoriented watching one screen move forward and the other backwards, so she turned her focus to the current screen. Cody would tell her if he found anything.

"Mako and some woman are in the hole," Cody said.

***

* * *

Mako opened his eyes and saw Hillary over him. "What happened? Where are we?" he asked.

"In a freaking hole. Are you okay?"

They were on a rough-hewn stone floor covered with several inches of standing water. Recoiling from the nastiness, he rose to his feet, fighting the dizziness, and stared up at the grate above their head. He extended his arms, trying to reach the wire, but he fell short. Maybe if he jumped, he thought, but then what?

"What are we going to do?" Hillary asked.

Mako looked up again and saw something circling above. It wasn't a bird. He stared at it and thought he heard a buzzing sound.

"It's a drone," Hillary said, standing behind him.

"Don't suppose it'll drop a line and pull us out." He looked back at their surroundings. There was nothing they could do here. The stone walls would be easy to climb, but then what? He would need some kind of leverage to lift the grate.

"I could stand on your shoulders and use the wall for support. See if that thing'll lift up," Hillary said.

She was reading his mind. He lowered his six-foot frame, set one knee in the water and used his hands to brace against the stone wall. Her feet dug into his back as she climbed onto him, but she was lighter than he expected and he rose slowly. Hillary was using her hands to stabilize them, and he adjusted to the feeling of her feet on his shoulders. He placed his hands on her ankles for support, almost forgetting their predicament when his hands touched her smooth skin.

Gunshots from above brought his attention back to the present. "Can you see anything?"

"Just keep walking around the walls. This side is embedded in the masonry, but the other side looks like it rests on top."

He shuffled his feet sideways, inching around the interior of the rectangular structure.

"Stop," she called.

They had just reached the midpoint of one of the long walls. He felt added weight on his shoulders but didn't dare look up.

"Turn around!"

He spun in a circle, and all of a sudden her weight was gone. Free to move now, he looked up and saw her use her elbow to prop the grate up while she slithered through.

"Give me your hand!" she called down to him.

She was on her belly with the grate resting on her back. Using the stone for a foothold, he extended himself and reached for her. He felt her grasp and felt the other hand grab his forearm. She was stronger than he expected, and she started lifting him out.

"You have to help," she called down.

He felt the grip loosen.

***

Storm crawled back into the building, trying to regain his bearings. His head pounded, making the pain in his shoulder seem like a pinprick. Dried blood covered one eye, but the other was unaffected. He got to his knees and peered around the corner. Something caught his eye and he turned to the left and saw Cyrus pulling the two cases out of the remains of the tower. *Crafty*, he thought, knowing he had underestimated his foes. Keeping the cases on the yacht could have been suicide, but why hide them here?

Just as he thought it, he heard the roar of an unmuffled engine and noticed a dust trail coming up the beach. It couldn't be coincidence, and he realized this was his last chance to stop them. He scanned the area and saw something move to his right near the helicopter. A quick look confirmed that Mei Lan had grabbed something from the cockpit and was heading to the road behind Cyrus. He had seconds to react, but just as he was about to go after them, he saw a body crawl out of the cistern. Hands reached out for the edge of the stone wall, but fell inches short. The torn pilot's uniform told him who it was. With only one eye, he swung his head back and forth, watching Cyrus and Mei Lan escape while Hillary struggled for her life. He left his cover and ran to the cistern, grabbing hold of her wrists just as she was about to slide back into the hole.

He pulled her out and looked down. On his belly he reached over the side, extended his arms and caught Mako's flailing hands. Together they pulled him free. The three of them were sprawled on the stone wall trying to catch their breath when he saw the drone hovering over him like it was trying to tell him something.

"Mako, find out who is flying that thing. I'll bet Alicia's got something to do with this," Storm said and went after the two figures moving toward the dust cloud.

***

"They're out and all alive," Alicia said and breathed in relief. "Tell him to focus on the other two," she told Cody.

"Ma'am, yes ma'am." He relayed the orders.

They both watched as the drone lifted into the air and sped toward the escaping duo. Cyrus and Mei Lan were a hundred feet apart when she saw the Iranian look over his shoulder. Mei Lan was gaining. They were moving along a rocky trail and he was slowed by the cases. Ahead, the trail looked like it went to the beach, and Alicia saw the dust cloud approach them. "What's that?"

"ATV or something. Running on the beach," Cody replied.

Just as she was about to reroute the drone to get a wider view, she saw Mei Lan overtake Cyrus. They ran together, but looked to be having a heated argument. "Keep an eye on them, we need a bigger picture," she said and moved her focus to the map of the island on the left-hand screen. The copper mine was at the tip of the island, and as she panned inland, she couldn't help but notice a road that ran dead straight and parallel to the beach. She stared at it, and all of a sudden it all made sense. It was a runway.

"Airport to the east of them. That's where they're headed."

"This is getting out of control. Maybe it's time to call the authorities," Cody said.

She had thought of that on many occasions and almost succumbed on several, but the incompetence of the locals might cost them the contract.

She recognized the voice. "Mako?" she called back to the speaker.

"SUP?"

She almost laughed at how cavalier he could be after facing death, but shook it off as she turned her attention to the screen with the drone's footage. "There's an airport. You have to get there before them."

CHAPTER 25

Mako turned to the drone operator and glanced at the cab behind them. "Well? You heard the lady. Can you take us to the airport?" he asked.

"It's a fare, man," he said and stuck his hand out. "Name's Al."

"Right on, man, you take plastic?" Mako asked.

He nodded and they hopped in the back of the cab. Al sped along the windy road ascending to the top of a small peak and made a hard right. The brakes screamed as he descended. This was taking too long, thought Mako, and he tapped on the rear window.

Al slid it open and the smell of the local ganja wafted back to him. "Where are we going?"

"It's the only way around the island, man," the driver said. He turned around but left the window open. The brakes squealed as they descended the winding road, a little too fast for Mako's preference, and entered a residential area. "I'll drop you at the end of this road here. You'll have a bit of a hike, though." The converted pickup reached the dead end, and they jumped off the back together.

"Hey. What about the fare?" Al screamed after them.

"The woman on the phone will take care of it," Mako yelled. Together he and Hillary jumped off the back of the open bed and stood on the dirt road, ignoring the curses of the driver as he pulled away. They stood frozen for a second, wondering what to do when, Mako saw an opening between two houses that led in the general direction they wanted to go. With no other options, they ran to the dirt trail. Making their way down the hill, tumbling when they hit loose rocks, they fought the low brush tearing at their clothes and exposed flesh. Slowly they made their way to the runway.

His stomach dropped when they reached it. He looked both ways and saw nothing. It was deserted—no planes, no ATVs, no people. He had expected to have to jump for the still-exposed landing gear of an escaping plane, pull himself aboard and save the day. But there was nothing here, and he stood on the hot tarmac waiting for an answer. Defeat surrounded him, and he turned toward Hillary. Just as he was about to confess his incompetence, he caught a small dust plume out of the corner of his eye. It was growing larger, coming from the direction of the copper mine. "We need some cover," Mako said.

"The hangar's over there." Hillary pointed to a metal building at the eastern end of the runway. "I've been in and out of here a few times."

They ran toward the building, hoping to get out of sight before the vehicle arrived. When their feet hit the tarmac, they were able to sprint the remaining distance—about half of the three-thousand-foot runway. Arriving exhausted, they stood in the shade of the open door, hands on their hips, trying to catch their breath. Once he had recovered, Mako started looking around and got an idea.

***

Storm half-stumbled and half-ran behind the ATV. The harsh

terrain quickly took a toll on his battered body, and he started falling behind. He chanced a look to sea and saw the Zodiac still trapped in the cove. As long as they were heading to the landing strip, this would be the perfect way to follow. Turning, he stumbled on a loose rock and felt his ankle cave underneath him. Pain shot through him, and he knew the boat was the only way. Unable to put any weight on the crippled leg, he crawled to the shore. The wind had died a bit, but the swells were still an issue as he slid down a large rock and into the water. The first thing he saw was a large wave coming toward the shore, which he ducked underneath to avoid its force. Surfacing, he used the backwash to help propel him to the Zodiac. Another wave crashed over him, but he had a firm hold on the rope strung around the gunwales. The soft sides of the boat cushioned the blow, helping him ride out the surge. Once it passed, he hauled himself over the edge and went to the helm.

After a brief fit, the engine fired and he turned the bow to the seas, timing his exit as a wave passed underneath the boat. He cleared the rocks, and the wave action settled into large, but more gentle rollers, allowing him to turn parallel to shore and follow the ATV. They were still going straight, following the rock-strewn beach. Steering slightly away from land to conceal both himself and the vessel if they chanced a look, he sped ahead.

As he approached, his mood darkened. The runway was graded a good twelve feet higher than the shore to protect it from storm surges, but the height gave him no vantage point to see what was going on there. He had to make a decision.

The buzz of a small plane caught his attention, and he looked to the west. A twin-propeller island hopper came into view and started its descent. The white fuselage with the blue tail fin struck something in his memory, and he recalled the Cape Air insignia from his flight to Tortola. The plane was close enough now to see the tail clearly, and the white bird on the blue background confirmed his guess.

This must be the aircraft that Cyrus and Mei Lan planned to escape on, he thought, and an idea began to form. But first he had to find Mako and Hillary. He gunned the motor, enduring the pain as the bow crashed into the seas. With some kind of resolution in sight, he ignored the throbbing in his shoulder and head. He needed to reach the hangar before the ATV.

He changed course toward shore and was able to easily land the boat on the beach by the runway. His feet hit the ground, and he immediately stumbled on his bad ankle. On all fours, he crawled up the embankment until his head was level with the tarmac. Fumes from the fueling shed across the way wafted across the runway on the breeze, making him cough and reminding him of the wound to his shoulder. He felt exposed, but there was no place to hide. Certainly nothing he could reach in his present condition. Crouching behind a small rock, he watched the plane land and taxi. As it passed, he tried to see if there were any passengers, but the tinted windows revealed nothing but the pilot, who had his door cracked to allow some ventilation into the cockpit.

The plane turned and stopped. He watched two attendants amble out of the hangar, jump into a golf cart with an extended bed and drive to the plane. The door opened and the pilot emerged. A strange look appeared on his face when he saw the attendants, but from this far away he couldn't hear what they were saying. He looked closer and realized it was Mako and Hillary. An unusual feeling permeated his chest, and he realized it was a little pride in his son's ingenuity.

The ATV was on the runway now, and he ducked low behind the

rock as it passed. He could see it clearly. A four-seat Gator with a pickup bed, three passengers hanging on to the roll bar and two cases banging against the sidewalls in the rear bed. It slowed at the plane, and the two passengers exited and stood off to the side. They appeared to be having a heated discussion while they waited for the driver to remove the cases.

***

Mako used the golf cart to hide them as he helped Hillary out of her jumpsuit. She did her best to smooth the wrinkles and cover the tears in her uniform blouse. He pushed her toward the ladder. If she was able to take the pilot's seat before Mei Lan and Cyrus boarded, they would likely never notice her. Mako helped her in and watched as she started her preflight. The other pilot had been amicable to the change. Their offer was hard to refuse: the remainder of the rental on the sailboat for swapping schedules. All he had to do was hop on a ferry and get to Jost Van Dyke.

Pulling the bill of his cap down and hunching over slightly, Mako used the fuselage to shield himself from the ATV. He crept around the rear of the aircraft and muttered something to the driver before taking the cases from him. Turning quickly away, he thought for a second about taking off and running, but realized he wouldn't get far. He opened the aft storage door and placed the cases into the baggage compartment. Then, making sure he wasn't observed, he jumped in behind them and pulled the door closed.

Crammed into the tight space, with his knees jammed into his chest, he had to keep his head bent in an uncomfortable position to avoid the low ceiling. He could hear conversation through the thin bulkhead separating the compartment from the passenger area and cockpit. Hillary was in the middle of a quick safety briefing. While she went through the standard spiel, he looked around the cargo area for anything that might help.

***

Storm watched the plane taxi and turn into the wind. The engines revved and the fuselage shimmied as the pilot increased the RPMs. Suddenly it stopped and the passenger door flew open. A body fell out, and he thought for a second it was Mako, but after studying the crumpled form's size and shape, he realized it was Cyrus. The door closed and the plane resumed its takeoff.

He had to do something to stop it. But he had no weapon. The gun was long gone. He reached into his pocket, looking for his phone, and pulled it out. The screen was shattered and water had seeped into the inner workings. Now with no communication or weapons, he felt helpless.

The plane was gaining speed as it moved down the runway. Just as it passed him, the wheels lifted and it was airborne. He looked back at Cyrus, who was on his knees now, signaling for the Gator to pick him up. The driver reached him and he crawled in. There had to be something he could do to stop it. Down, but not defeated, he rose and started to limp toward the hangar, trying to figure out how to reach Alicia. Maybe they would have a phone, an old-fashioned phone with a cord—one that worked. He was about to cross the runway when he saw the Gator coming toward him, and instinctively he dove for cover.

He watched it retrace its path, looking like it was heading back to the mine, and he changed plans. With the Zodiac, he could get there before the Gator and ambush Cyrus. He crawled down the bank to the beach and grabbed the side of the Zodiac. Pushing it was hard with only one working foot, but he waited for the right wave and put everything he had left into it. The hard bottom ground on the rocks and he jumped in.

Seconds later, he had the boat turned and was retracing his route to the mine, the Gator running just ahead of him.

CHAPTER 26

The force of the plane taking off pushed Mako against the bulkhead separating the baggage compartment from the small passenger area. He could feel it move and reached over to touch the thin plastic barrier. Breaking through it would be all good, except he had no idea what lay on the other side. He suspected it was only Mei Lan and Hillary. From the fracas that had occurred before they took off, he assumed Cyrus was not on board.

The plane banked hard to starboard, and he used his legs to brace against the fuselage. The ride quickly leveled off, and he searched the bulkhead for any opening he could use to observe the cabin. He found a small pinhole where a now-missing screw or bolt had once helped secure the partition. It was awkward, but with the turbulence and noise of the engines, he didn't need to disguise his movements. Finally, he managed to rearrange his body to allow him to peer through the small opening. Mei Lan was the only passenger, and she was sitting in the rear starboard seat. He squirmed for a better view and saw the gun in her hand. Mako tried to piece a timeline together for the flight. He knew it was short, but had spent much of his time on the flight over flirting with Hillary. Suddenly, the nose of the plane dipped, and he knew if he was going to pull this off, he would have to act quickly.

It was an effort to turn inside the small compartment, especially with the two cases, but he finally managed to spin himself so his back was to the rear of the plane. Hoping that Hillary would keep her composure, he pulled his legs back as tight as they would go to his chest, hoping he would be able to generate enough force within the cramped compartment to kick in the bulkhead.

In his head, he counted down from there. On the count of one, he felt the plane shift slightly and bank to port. They must be on their final approach. With no time to waste, he pulled his knees tight to his chest and kicked the hard plastic barrier with both feet. He had aimed on the left side, knowing that Mei Lan was on the right and the bulkhead folded into the cabin.

He didn't know if Hillary was reacting to him or if it was part of the landing, but the plane banked hard to starboard, the G force of the turn pushing Mei Lan into the window. Mako tried to use the advantage to take her, but the thin plastic material that comprised the bulkhead was stuck on his legs. He squirmed, trying to get it off, kicking his legs to free himself, but before he could turn, Mei Lan had figured out what was happening and had the gun pointed at him.

"You're not going to shoot me in a pressurized cabin," Mako said, as calmly as he could.

"Idiot," was all she said.

Mako saw the look in her eye and froze, knowing she really intended to shoot. Hillary must have sensed it as well. She pulled the yoke back, and the plane went into a sharp climb. The G force took Mei Lan by surprise, and Mako had his chance.

His legs were still stuck in the material, but he was able to swing them into her. The gun fell from her hands as the torn plastic cut into her. With his back against the opposite side of the fuselage, he used his long frame and the leverage he had to pin her against the window.

"I've got to get back on the flight plan," Hillary said. She turned around and grabbed the gun from the floor. "It'll take about five minutes to get us on the ground. Can you hold her?"

"Got it, boss. You just fly," Mako said.

Hillary resumed her descent, and Mako focused everything he had on keeping Mei Lan under restraint. The plane banked again, causing him to shift, but his tall frame was firmly lodged between the rear and front seat.

"Let me know what you're up to," he said.

"Landing in three minutes," Hillary said.

Now he had to decide what to do once they landed.

***

Storm was hurting. Every wave jarred him as the Zodiac plowed into the seas, each one causing him to wince in pain. The Gator was heading back to the mine with Cyrus, but he had no idea why. The ruins came into view first, and the road started to gain elevation. Then he saw the rotor of the helicopter. He dropped speed and relaxed slightly as the pounding stopped and he watched the Gator climb. Nearing the cove where he had beached before, he realized that from the clearing where the chopper sat, they would have a clear view of him. Coming up the cliffs would take Cyrus by surprise, but he wasn't sure his body could make the ascent. With no alternative plan, he followed the coast past the cove to thc steeper cliffs. Hoping his injured ankle, now swollen to the size of a grapefruit, would allow him to climb, he steered for the most hospitable spot on the shore.

There was nowhere to safely beach the boat, so he cut the engine and allowed the wave action to bring him close to the rocks. Moving to the bow, he readied himself and jumped into the water just before the nose of the Zodiac hit a large boulder. The water cushioned his exit, and he pulled himself onto land. Crawling on his belly, he worked hand and foot to ascend the rocky grade. With little weight on his ankle, he was surprised at the ease which he climbed. Once he reached the top, he crawled over and kneeled behind a cluster of rocks.

The Gator was parked by the helicopter, the driver waiting patiently while Cyrus searched the cockpit. Storm sat and watched, wondering what he was up to, when he turned with a smile on his face and the laptop in his hand. Not sure how the playing field had changed after the fight with Mei Lan back at the runway, he knew one thing for certain—Cyrus had the encryption code. He was back in the Gator now, and Storm reacted out of instinct. Had he waited and thought about it, he might not have made the leap that had him dragging from the back bumper of the ATV.

Neither the driver nor Cyrus had seen him stumble from the cover of the rocks and launch himself toward the Gator. With his legs dragging behind, he grabbed onto the tailgate and held on. It was easier than he expected, with the vehicle moving slowly to navigate through the minefield of rocks. Slowly he used the up-and-down motion of the shocks as they bounced over the rocky terrain to lift himself into the bed of the vehicle.

Cyrus must have felt his weight and turned. The look of surprise was clear on his face, and Storm took the seconds he had before he reacted to reach for a garden hoe lying in the bed. He wound up and released a blow towards Cyrus's head, but the Gator hit another rock and he missed, the sharp tool embedding itself in the dashboard. Sprawled over the seat trying to wrench the hoe free, Cyrus had the advantage, but was weaponless. He used the laptop to deliver a blow to the back of Storm's head, but again the terrain foiled the attack. The hard edge of the case grazed Storm's ear, but there was no force behind it. Cyrus was flung forward as a result of the attempt, and Storm half-crawled onto him, using the other man's body for leverage. With both hands, he pulled and the hoe released.

He exchanged glances with the driver, who appeared confused. Storm felt him brake, causing the men to become tangled together, their closeness not allowing Storm to wind up and deliver the blow that he would have liked. Unable to use the business end of the hoe, he lifted the round wooden handle straight up and slammed the butt hard into Cyrus's head. Something gave way. The end entered the other man's skull, and Storm could feel him go limp.

The Gator was on the beach road, the driver looking straight ahead as if this might never have happened if he didn't look.

"Stop and we'll dump the body. No one needs to know," Storm said.

The man's face didn't change, but he listened and stopped the Gator by the water. Storm glanced over to see if he would help, but he stared straight ahead. Hobbling, Storm slid out of the opening and pulled the body behind him onto the rocks. He checked his pockets for anything that might prove useful and took his cell phone and wallet before hauling the body to the water's edge. He debated whether to weight the body with rocks, but decided to just cast it unceremoniously into the surf.

He stood watching for several minutes as the waves took the body out to sea. It was soon invisible, and he turned back to the driver. "Can you run me back to the airport?"

Still looking straight ahead, the driver put the ATV in gear and nodded. Storm stumbled back to the Gator, climbed into the passenger seat and grasped the laptop as the driver started back to the airport.

***

Hillary landed and taxied the plane to the Cape Air gate. “Here they are,” she said.

After she was sure that Mako had Mei Lan restrained, she had radioed for the police to meet the plane, saying that there was an unruly passenger. Two policemen approached the plane with their hands on their holsters, not knowing what to expect. They separated, each moving to cover each door. Hillary opened the cockpit door, extending her hands so they could see she was unarmed.

“She’s in the back. Another passenger has her restrained,” she said, remaining in the plane.

They moved together to the other side of the plane and released the latch on the door. Mako gave a shove as it released and Mei Lan fell to the ground. They lifted the helpless woman to her feet.

“My ID is in my back pocket. You might want to check it before you do something stupid. Something that could end your meaningless careers.”

Mako and Hillary exchanged glances, not knowing what she was up to. The officers looked at each other and one bent down.

“Don’t touch me,” she screeched and reached into her pocket.

Mako saw the crimson color of the passport before it was fully out and knew she would walk away.

* * *

***

Mako and Hillary had been escorted directly from the plane to an FBI holding area in the main terminal. For the last fifteen minutes, they had sat silently in a sterile room with a desk and three chairs, waiting to discover their fate. One policeman had remained with them and the other had escorted Mei Lan away. Mako would remember the look on her face for a long time after this was over. It was as close to pure hatred as he had ever seen.

Their IDs had been taken when they were put in the room, and they could do nothing but sit in an uncomfortable silence and wait. Finally the door opened and the stereotypical bureau agent walked in.

"You checked out, and the uranium is secured. I guess we owe you a thank-you if this doesn't turn into an international incident with the Chinese woman. There was nothing we could do except release her once she flashed the diplomatic passport."

He was concise and professional, but Mako got the feeling he really didn't care. "What about us?"

"The Agency vouched for you."

"So, we are free to go?" Mako asked.

"Yes, with our gratitude," he said, in a monotone voice that expressed disdain.

"What about my job?" Hillary asked.

"Cape Air has been informed about your service to the country. Don't expect you'll get a thank-you or promotion. We had to be a little sparse on the details."

She got up and walked to the door. Mako followed her, wondering if he should shake the agent's hand or not. He had an image of the guy pulling it back and smoothing his hair, like the cool dude in high school, so he just walked by him.

They stood outside the terminal, neither knowing what to do.

"Do you want…?" she started and he nodded.

"First, I need to touch base with Alicia."

CHAPTER 27

They stood by the pay phone in the terminal. "I'm sorry, this is going to be goodbye," Mako said. "Storm turned up with the computer, and I have to get back to Key Largo and see if we can still salvage our contract."

"Goodbye just for now, I hope," she said.

He reached for her and they pulled together in an embrace. Their lips met and they kissed deeply, the passion of their life-and-death struggle releasing. Finally they broke off, and he headed for the main terminal, hoping there would be a quick resolution and he could get back and see her. It was not lost on him how unusual this feeling was. He looked back, but she was gone.

Alicia had set him up with a flight to Miami, and he walked aimlessly to the gate. He was exhausted and should have been hungry, but the airport food did not entice him. Passing a bar, he thought about slamming a few cocktails, but even that didn't hold his interest. He had the feeling that his life was somehow changing.

***

They sat around the kitchen table, a plate of stone crabs in the center and a cold beer in front of each of them. Storm looked a little worse for the wear and still limped. Mako had slept, and though he felt an emptiness in his gut, he was otherwise alright. Cody had a hammer in his hand, demonstrating how to crack the hard shell of the crab claws. Mako ate, but didn't really taste the food.

"You okay there?" Storm asked. "Awful quiet."

"Yeah, I'm good," Mako said and took a swig of the beer to make it look like he was. "Just want to get this over with."

"And get back to your lady friend down south," Storm added for him.

"What's this?" Alicia asked.

There were a few laughs at his expense, which he let pass over his head, as Storm told the story of the budding romance. Fortunately the crab was almost finished and Alicia cleared the table.

"I'm going to work on Cyrus's computer now and see if I can pull the code off. Then we can wrap this up," Alicia said and left for the war room.

Mako and Storm said goodnight and headed off to the guest bedroom. They were barely settled in when Cody came to the door.

"Alicia needs you," he said and left.

They followed him into the dark room and stared at the screens. Lines of code flew across them, and Mako looked over at Alicia working frantically.

"Got it," she said with a look of relief. "Just thought I ought to let you know."

"Cool," Mako said. "We're done, then?"

"Not so fast. We have to get the code back to Lloyd's," she said.

"Well, shoot it on over the airwaves. I'm going to bed," he said, thinking that with this wrapped up sometime tomorrow, he could be on a beach with Hillary.

"Not so fast, lover boy," Alicia said. "This needs to be delivered by hand. It's way too risky to go over the Internet."

Shit, Mako thought. Well, a couple of days and he'd be on that beach—and with a pocket full of money. "Okay, I'll be heading out tomorrow, then."

"Again, not so fast. Red-eye leaves Miami in a few hours. Sorry, you can sleep on the plane."

He resigned himself to his fate, not really upset about the night flight. The sooner he got there, the sooner he would return.

"One thing, though," Alicia said. "Mei Lan is still unaccounted for. I lost her trail in Puerto Rico."

Now Mako had something to think about. The woman wouldn't go away.

***

Three hours later, he settled into his seat. The flight was only three-quarters full, and he was able to relax with an empty seat between him and a businessman who was already asleep. The flight attendant had just made the announcement to turn off all portable electronic devices, and he reached for his phone when it lit up with a text. *Mei Lan is in London.* The simple mission had just gotten much more difficult.

Sleep didn't come. Unable to get Hillary from his mind, and now having to deal with Mei Lan, even the flight attendant, a very attractive brunette, couldn't distract him. They had just started their descent when he realized he hadn't even flirted with her.

It was late morning when he arrived in London, the time change eating up much of the night. Mako walked off the plane and headed to the tube station to catch the express into the city. He walked through the terminal, knowing he should be checking faces, but he was tired and distracted.

The platform was already crowded when he got off the long escalator. Staying to the edge, he walked toward the rear and waited. The train pulled into the station, releasing the incoming passengers through the opposite doors. Once they were out, the doors opened and he followed the mass of people into the car. Settling into his seat for the twenty-minute ride, he put the earwig in his ear and adjusted the bone mike by his throat. Tapping the mike, he heard Alicia's reassuring voice in his ear. He knew she would know where he was by his cell phone's GPS, so he didn't need to say anything.

He had an uneasy feeling that someone was watching him, and not being able to sit still, he got up and started moving into the forward cars. At least he could beat the crowds off. Each car became progressively more crowded as the aggressive commuters made to be the first off. He fought through them and made his way to the front of the train. Soon people were standing by the doors, with others making their way towards the rear, where they might find a seat. Deciding to stay where he was, he turned sideways to allow an attractive woman he might have ordinarily flirted with to pass by, when he saw her.

Without hesitating for another look, he turned and headed to the back of the train.

"She's here," he whispered into the mike.

"Mei Lan?"

"No, the tooth fairy. Of course."

"Sorry, I'll start running options. Did she see you?" Alicia asked.

"I don't think so," Mako said, moving past another group of people crowded around the door area.

"Okay. Running scenarios to get you out of there." He took every opportunity he could to look back, but there was still a stream of passengers, and he couldn't see more than a few feet behind him. It didn't help that she was short as well as crafty. She could blend in and become invisible. He reached the last car and thought he had escaped observation when the train slowed and a voice came over the speaker announcing that the train was entering the station. Not wanting to wait for the crowd, he made his way to the rear and opened the door to the narrow platform outside the car.

CHAPTER 28

Mako timed his jump for the exact moment when the car would reach the concrete platform. The train was still moving, but he needed every second he could get. He landed badly on the concrete, but ignored the shooting pain in his knee and ran down the tracks, away from the terminal. Risking a glance behind him, he saw Mei Lan exit the train and look both ways. He thought he had evaded her, but she must have seen him and followed. Thankful for the crowd between them, he jumped onto the rubble next to the tracks and ran toward daylight. The glass-domed vault covering the station ended abruptly, and the first drops of rain hit him. “What now?” he almost screamed into his mike.

“You’ve got about eight blocks and I think we can make you disappear,” Alicia said.

Mako was not so sure as he looked around. People surrounded him, but he knew Mei Lan would not be easy to lose.

“Continue on Cleveland Street. It will veer to the left and turn into Leinster Gardens,” she said.

He ran through the crowded streets, limping slightly on his bad leg.

“Almost there,” Alicia said. “Look for numbers twenty-three and twenty-four on the right.”

"And then you make me disappear?" Mako panted the words. The house numbers were going down, and he knew he was close to whatever she was leading him into. "I see it."

"Go past to the next alley and see if you can find a way behind them."

"Behind?"

"They are false fronts. There is a section of tube tunnel open behind them." The open space was a remnant of another era, when vents were needed in the underground shafts to release the toxic fumes from the coal-burning locomotives. Numbers 23 and 24 Leinster Gardens were one of several false-fronted buildings that still remained around the world.

"If you say so." He was almost to the corner when he saw the scaffolding. If he needed to get behind the houses, the fastest way might not be around, but up and over. He reversed course and saw Mei Lan at the corner. She had stopped and was searching the street for him. Fortunately she had to be cautious and check each storefront. The businesses were all open, and he could have ducked into any of them to throw her off. Pausing at the first upright, he estimated the height and launched his body with his hand extended like Superman. He just reached the lowest section and grabbed the slick aluminum tube with his hands. Swinging like a gymnast, he gathered enough momentum to access the next level and reached a ladder. The going was easier now, but he was totally exposed and risked a glance down at the street.

The street below him was crowded with pedestrians grouped around the building, staring up at him as if this was some sort of performance. Cursing himself, he knew he should have taken Alicia's advice and gone around back, but here he was: three stories above the street. The crowd stood below, staring at him as he climbed over the parapet wall and saw the ruse.

Below him, two sets of steel girders spanned the distance between the two adjacent buildings. If he could reach the lower ones, he would be able to land on top of the next train. The rain came in sheets now, making the climbing more difficult, but there were footholds built into the backside of the false-fronted built-indings to allow access for the workers. He was over the wall now and climbed down to the first beam. Just as he was about to swing to the lower girder, a bullet struck the steel. The vibration echoed through his whole body, but he clung to the wet steel and lowered himself to the next foothold.

The spectators must have aroused her suspicion, and Mei Lan was on the parapet wall. However, as long as he stayed against the building, she would not have a clear shot. He reached the second set of beams just ten feet off the ground and stared back into the tunnel. "Next train is due?" he whispered into the mike.

"Two minutes," Alicia responded.

"Don't suppose you could push that up any?" Mako said. It was too long for him to just stand here like an ordinary suit waiting for their commuter train. Mei Lan would be on him in seconds. He looked up and saw her coming down. Just a few more steps and she would have an easy shot. He looked around for any way to avoid her. Even with the low visibility of the storm, the courtyard was totally exposed, and without a weapon he was helpless. The dark tunnel beckoned.

He crouched and leapt just as her foot reached the hold above him. Landing on the ground with a thud and rolling forward, he looked up, but the beam obscured her. Just as he was about to make a run across the courtyard to the protection of the tunnel, he heard the rumble of the train. The light was just visible, and he veered away from the tunnel to the opposite track.

Bullets hit the rubble around his feet, and he looked up. Hoping the steel structure would obscure him, he started climbing the electric and gas pipes that were fastened horizontally to the wall. "How much longer?"

"I can't tell. It's got to be close—it looks like it's right on top of you."

Mako clung to the pipe as bullets smashed into the old brick around him. Frozen against the wall, his feet clinging to the old conduits, he counted the seconds. The train was almost past, but his grip was slipping. He reached up, trying to grab a better handhold below the beam, but fell short, the movement causing his feet to slip on the wet pipes. The train emerged from the tunnel and sped past him, its jet stream almost pulling him from the wall. The last car finally passed, and he was about to release his grip and drop to the ground when he saw Mei Lan crouching on the tracks.

From the tunnel, a deep rumble from the other direction caught his attention. A plan was forming in his head, but he had only seconds to act.

"Hand over the drive," she yelled.

He ignored her, saving his energy. Perched on the largest conduit attached to the wall, he looked down and saw several other smaller pipes above it, but they were clearly not large enough to hold him. Reaching up again, his hand fell several inches from the girder. The gun fired again, and mortar flew from a brick near his head. He knew he was out of time.

"Drop it now," she screamed.

"You've got to do better than that," he panted and started to climb. With a quick look over his shoulder, he saw her coming after him. She was halfway across the yard when he turned away.

The movement caused him to miss the next handhold, and he started to fall backwards. Regaining his balance, he forced himself back against the wall and started climbing. The ground vibrated and the sound grew louder. He sensed the train, but didn't dare to look in case she followed his eyes and saw his intent. Using the pipes like rungs on a ladder, he scampered up the vertical wall, his momentum carrying him within reach of the beam. He wasted no time and pulled himself onto the steel girder just as the first car emerged from the tunnel. He looked down. The train was blasting through the open area. He clung to the wall, waiting for it to pass. It never slowed, and after it disappeared into the opposite tunnel, he looked down at the line of fresh blood on the rubble between the tracks.

"Any chatter about the train?" he whispered into the bone mike.

"Nothing. What happened?" Alicia asked.

He didn't answer.

***

Mako discarded the earwig and bone mike as he walked the half dozen blocks to the Lloyd's building. The rain had stopped. Though the cloud cover was still heavy, he could see the sun trying to break free as it rose higher in the sky. Despite the last few days, he was feeling upbeat, appreciating the women walking by dressed for the summer heat. The Lloyd's building appeared as he rounded a corner, and he couldn't help but retrace in his mind the steps he had used to escape.

He approached the building in a different frame of mind than the last time he was here. A white-gloved doorman greeted him by name and opened the door. A woman in a tight-fitting business suit came up and shook his hand, ignoring his leering smile as she led him to the elevators. The doors opened, revealing the same set of cubicles that he had snuck through less than a week ago. They were full now, and the woman cleared her throat.

"Ladies and gentlemen. Please say hello to Mr. Storm," she said.

As one, they rose and applauded. Grinning, he looked at the woman. "I'm Mako. My father is Mr. Storm."

She tried to contain the laugh. He must have spoken louder than he thought, because soon the entire room was laughing. Soon all the workers were approaching him to shake hands and congratulate him on saving the reputation of the prestigious firm. He thanked them and handed the drive to the lead programmer, who clutched his hand, a bit harder than expected, and thanked him profusely. The woman cleared her throat several times in a distinctly British fashion, and soon the room was back to normal.

"Well, Mr. Storm—I mean Mako. Lloyd's extends a sincere thank-you for all you have done."

He smiled at her. "And the contract payment?"

"Right. We'll take a detour through accounting on the way out," she said.

"And then what?" he asked and put his hand on the small of her back just as the elevator doors opened.

"I'm afraid I don't know what you mean," she said.

He saw the look in her eye and moved closer. "But I think you do." He leaned in to kiss her, but before he could brush her lips, he pulled away. She gave him a questioning look, but he just stared at the door.

***

* * *

They were anchored in twenty feet of water just north of Key Largo. Mako expertly popped the cork on the champagne and poured it into the waiting glasses. They raised them and nodded an unspoken toast.

"No word from your dad?" Alicia asked.

"Nope. Dropped off the grid. Something he's good at," Mako said.

Silence prevailed for a few seconds.

Hillary whispered in Mako's ear, "I want to get wet."

Alicia helped her into the dive gear. She gave her the rundown on the equipment and a brief safety talk. This would be the woman's first time on SCUBA, but Alicia had done the Discover Diving briefing many times. Taking people out for their first underwater experience was one of the things she really enjoyed, and she still remembered when Cody had taken her on their first date.

Mako watched from the deck, champagne glass in hand. When the two women had disappeared below the surface, he turned to Cody, who was playing a game on his phone. Leaving him to his amusement, Mako climbed up to the bridge and sat on the bench seat behind the helm, staring at the bubbles from the two divers and smiling.

Made in the USA
Lexington, KY
05 June 2016